"Don't you care
for me at all?"

Jarod's laugh was harsh. "I want you Amanda," he replied. "I want you the same way I've wanted dozens of women."

His brutal honesty stunned her. "You don't feel any difference with me?" She raised pain-filled eyes to his face.

"What difference could there be?" Jarod mocked.

"Love!"

"You're a sentimental fool," he jeered. "Love is just another word for lust. When the physical attraction wears off, you'll find you don't love me, either."

"My love for you isn't a dream that will fade in the morning," Amanda spoke softly, but surely. "I thought I had no pride where you're concerned, Jarod. But if all you feel for me is desire, I never want to see you again."

JANET DAILEY AMERICANA

Janet Dailey
Americana

NIGHT OF
THE COTILLION

Harlequin Books

TORONTO • NEW YORK • LONDON
AMSTERDAM • PARIS • SYDNEY • HAMBURG
STOCKHOLM • ATHENS • TOKYO • MILAN

The state flower depicted on the cover of this book is
Cherokee rose.

Janet Dailey Americana edition published October 1986
Second printing May 1988
Third printing May 1989
Fourth printing May 1990
Fifth printing June 1991

ISBN 373-89860-6

Harlequin Presents edition published March 1977
Second printing June 1979
Third printing February 1982

Original hardcover edition published in 1976
by Mills & Boon Limited

Printed in U.S.A.

CHAPTER ONE

"THANKS FOR THE RIDE, Tobe," said Amanda, bending down to peer in the car window, the scarlet sheen of her hair burning brightly in the rays of the late-afternoon sun.

"Be sure to have Brad call me tonight." He nodded as he gunned the engine and shifted the car into reverse.

"Will do," she promised. "See you!"

With a wave of her hand she turned toward the house, smiling to herself as she imagined her mother grimacing at the way Tobe Peterson had roared down the street. No matter how many times her mother reprimanded him for driving so carelessly, he still did it—mostly, Amanda thought, to annoy her mother who treated Tobe like one of her own sons. Amanda was convinced that was the very reason he spent so much of his time at their house, because he felt a part of their family. Tobe and her brother Brad had been inseparable friends since their first day of kindergarten.

The Petersons had large cotton holdings, exceeded only by those owned by Colby Enterprises, but Tobe's supposedly superior status in the community didn't interest him one bit. All of the Bennetts, including Amanda, tended to forget who his family was. His clothes and car were more expensive than theirs, and that seemed to be the only difference.

She took the porch steps two at a time, swinging open the screen door of the large, two-story house and letting it slam behind her. "Mom! I'm home!"

"Sssh!" Her mother appeared in the dining-room archway. "Your grandfather is taking a nap."

"I was," came a grumpy voice, "until that young fool blasted out of the driveway."

"That was Tobe," Amanda announced unnecessarily. "He gave me a ride home. Don't let me forget—he wants Brad to call him tonight." She walked swiftly to the elderly man who appeared in the doorway, his broad shoulders stooped with the weight of his advanced age. "Hello, grandpa," planting a kiss on his leathered cheek. "How are you today?"

"Ah, my hip is acting up on me again," he grumbled, but his eyes were twinkling as he looked at his granddaughter. "Must be going to have a change in the weather."

"There's lemonade in the refrigerator," her mother spoke up.

"Sounds great. Does anyone else want a glass?" Amanda called over her shoulder as her long legs carried her toward the kitchen.

"Not me." Her grandfather shook his head.

"I'll have one." And her mother followed her out to the kitchen. "How did it go today?"

"Hectic," Amanda sighed, removing two

glasses from the cupboard and the ice tray and pitcher of lemonade from the refrigerator. "For a while this afternoon I was almost wishing the term wasn't over and I was still taking the end-of-term exams."

"Please don't wish that on me," her mother laughed, shaking her dark auburn hair, which was just beginning to be streaked with gray. "With all three of your brothers and yourself in college and Bonnie in high school and all your final tests falling within the same week, I don't know if your dad and I can live through that again."

"It was pretty wild around here, wasn't it?" Amanda smiled, a tiny dimple appearing in each cheek. "All of us burning the midnight oil and fighting over the typewriter to get term papers done. I guess the pace was a bit more frantic. But teaching three new girls the ropes out at Oak Run is a little nerve-racking too."

"I'm rather proud that Mrs. Matthews put you in charge of training them. Usually she insists on doing it herself."

"I've been a guide there since I was seventeen. That's more than four years. I know as much about the plantation as she does. Besides, she's all wrapped up in the plans for the cotillion. Which was another reason things got out of hand today. She was there with the florist trying to decide what flowers should go where, et cetera."

"Talking about the cotillion," Mrs. Bennett inserted, "let's go and try on your dress. I tacked it together this morning. We can see how it fits and get the hemline pinned. Leave your lemonade here," she ordered quickly as Amanda started to walk out of the kitchen with the glass in her hand. "Don't bring it into the sewing room. I don't want to spill anything on that taffeta material."

"Are they having that dance at Oak Run?" her grandfather mumbled as they walked through the dining room toward the small room Bernice Bennett used as a sewing room.

"They do every year, grandpa," Amanda answered, exchanging a knowing look with her mother.

"Jeff Davis would turn over in his grave if he knew," he declared angrily. "It's an outright crime to celebrate his birthday in that damn Yankee's house!"

"It's a tradition, grandpa Bennett," her mother replied soothingly. "And Oak Run was a Confederate home long before Colonel Colby bought it."

"That makes no difference! A Yankee owns it now. They should find somewhere else to hold their cotillion."

"Oh, grandpa," Amanda scolded teasingly, wrinkling her nose at his long-held dislike of anyone born north of the Mason-Dixon line. "If it weren't for Mrs. Matthews and the Colby money, there wouldn't be any cotillion. Try to forget who owns the plantation and remember that we're celebrating the birthday of the former president of the Confederate States in a fine old southern home. The way you carry on sometimes about Yankees, a person would think you'd fought in the Civil War yourself."

"My grandpappy did!" he answered testily, his

dark brows gathering together in a thunderous frown. "Many's the time he sat me on his knee and told me stories about the burning of Atlanta and the way Sherman's army raped and pillaged the land on their way to Savannah."

"All that happened more than a hundred years ago, too," Mrs. Bennett reminded him. "And it's best forgotten."

"Nobody's forgotten, nobody in Georgia, least-ways. If they had, you wouldn't be having any cotillion to celebrate Jeff Davis's birthday," he retorted smugly.

Mrs. Bennett lifted her shoulders in an expressive shrug toward her daughter and Amanda smiled. There wasn't any reasoning with her grandfather. There was the North and the South, and if he had his way, never the twain should meet.

"Come on, Amanda," her mother waved to her. "Let's try that dress on."

Amanda followed her into the sewing room while her grandfather began whistling "Dixie" as loud as he could. "The old reprobate," Amanda said smiling. Then her eyes saw the gown on the dressmaker's form. "Mom, it's beautiful!" she breathed.

"You'll have to put the hoops on so I can make sure it hangs right. I don't think it will matter if you don't have the petticoats on."

Eagerly Amanda stripped down to her under-wear and stepped into the wide-hooped underskirt while her mother carefully removed the old-fashioned-style ball gown from the form and placed it over her daughter's head. She stood impatiently while her mother put in the essential pins to keep it on, then dashed to the full-length mirror.

"You are a genius, mom," Amanda vowed. But while she was admiring her reflection, Bernice Bennett was frowning in dissatisfaction as she put in a tuck here and there.

"With six children to clothe and feed and send to college, I'd better know how to sew to save money," she murmured, adjusting the shoulder straps designed as mock sleeves. "I doubt if we could have afforded to buy you a gown to go to the cotillion."

"I would rather have this gown than any you could buy," Amanda answered fervently. "I look like a genuine Southern belle."

The material was a rich green that shimmered from emerald brilliance to deep forest shades where the many folds draped over the hoops to her small waist. It artfully molded her breasts while setting off her ivory cream skin and the red gold of her hair.

"The neckline is a bit too low," her mother declared.

"No, it's not," Amanda protested. Her liquid brown eyes beamed at her mother with impish mirth. "It's a bit daring, maybe, but if it were any higher, I'd look like a Puritan."

"You would look like a proper young lady," her mother replied. The front screen door slammed. "Is that you, Brad?" Mrs. Bennett called, turning briefly away from her daughter. "I'm in the sewing room."

"Is Amanda there?" her brother answered, his voice coming nearer. "Cheryl is with me."

"I'm in here, Cheryl," Amanda answered, "trying on my gown for the cotillion."

The dark-haired girl appeared in the doorway with a tall, lanky young man hovering behind her. Her eyes widened as she saw Amanda.

"Oh, Mrs. Bennett, you didn't make that, did you?" Cheryl exclaimed. "It's gorgeous! With that beautiful red hair of yours fixed back in ringlets, you'll look fantastic, Amanda! What a shame you don't have green eyes!"

"Amanda wouldn't want to trade in her spaniel eyes," her brother teased. "She enjoys having men drown in those liquid pools of brown."

"I wish I could drown you!" she threatened.

"Hush, you two!" their mother intervened. "And hold still, Amanda, so I can pin this neckline."

Amanda tilted her head in mock sorrow to Cheryl. "Mom thinks the neckline is too low."

"Oh, no, Mrs. Bennett, don't raise it," the dark-haired girl protested. "These old gowns always had some cleavage showing."

"This gown will have a quarter of an inch less cleavage," her mother stated emphatically. "That's all I can gain without ruining the line."

"I wish I didn't have a tan," Cheryl sighed. "I can't figure out what I'm going to do to cover the white streaks where my swimming-suit straps were. I'm going to have to experiment and see if I can cover it up with makeup."

"All done," Mrs. Bennett announced. "Why don't you two run out to the kitchen while Amanda changes? There's lemonade in the refrigerator and cookies in the jar."

"Hurry, Mandy," Cheryl urged. "I just found out the most fantastic thing. I'm dying to tell you."

"I'll be right there."

"Careful," her mother admonished. "It's only tacked."

Once the gown was off and safely on its form, Amanda scurried into her slacks and top. "I love it, mom. Maybe when Tobe sees me in it, it will make up for the fact that his parents are making him go to the cotillion."

"I think it was sweet of him to ask you to go."

"Heaven knows, I've talked about it enough." Amanda grinned. "It's been my dream to be invited to it. I consider myself lucky that Tobe is between girl friends right now."

"He certainly plays the field," her mother agreed with a wry smile. "You'd better hurry out to the kitchen before Cheryl forgets what it is that she's 'dying' to tell you."

With the remains of a smile still curving her mouth, Amanda hurried toward the kitchen. Cheryl did tend to exaggerate and overreact, but they had always been close friends and had become even more so since Cheryl had started dating Brad. For all the comments made about her gossiping tongue, if Cheryl were entrusted with a secret, she would keep it to her dying day. And there were many secrets shared between them.

"Here I am," Amanda stated, walking into the

kitchen where Cheryl and Brad were sitting at the table. "What were you going to tell me?"

"Sit down, sit down." Cheryl motioned toward the chair beside her, which Amanda took. "Well, you know that Colby Enterprises transferred their computer and data-processing operations to Atlanta last year, and their electronics plant here in Oak Springs will be completed in June—next month."

"Yes, everybody knows that." Amanda tilted her head inquiringly toward the brunette.

"Here's something that most people don't know." Cheryl paused to add suspense. "Rumor has it that Jarod Colby is moving to Georgia permanently. More specifically, he's going to take up residence in Oak Springs at the Winter House."

"Are you sure?" Amanda's heart gave a funny little leap. A mask swept over her face to conceal the fleeting twinge of excitement.

"Positive." Cheryl made the motion of crossing her heart. "It's even been said that he's giving up his directorship in that steel company in Pennsylvania. He's centralized all his companies here in Georgia. And—are you ready for this—" Cheryl leaned closer. "He's going to be the official host at the cotillion this year!"

"Now that I find hard to believe," Amanda said dryly.

"Supposedly he's going to announce his decision to live here permanently."

"He might as well," Brad said with a derisive laugh. "He practically owns the whole town. I suppose when we're introduced to him at the dance, we'll be required to bow in his royal presence."

"Who's that?" Grandfather Bennett demanded as he limped into the kitchen to catch the last of Brad's statement.

"Jarod Colby, who else?" he replied.

"Why would you be introduced to that Yankee carpetbagger?"

"He's going to be at the cotillion," Cheryl explained, darting a sparkling glance at Amanda. "Isn't it exciting?"

"Humph!" her grandfather snorted. "If it was me meeting him, I'd spit in his eye."

"Considering the fact that dad manages his cotton mill, it's a good thing you don't meet him, granddad," Brad chided.

"And if I was your dad, I'd still spit in his eye and find me a better job where I wasn't working for no Yankee!"

"Just think, Amanda," said Cheryl, lowering her voice to a whisper. "You're finally going to get to meet him!"

Once Amanda would have been a quivering mass of jelly at that prospect, but that was a long time ago.

"It doesn't matter so much anymore," she answered her friend, shrugging her shoulders to show her indifference.

Cheryl gasped before a knowing smile appeared on her face. "You don't mean that!"

"I do," Amanda nodded firmly.

"What are you two whispering about?" Brad broke in.

"We're talking about the dance," Cheryl fibbed. "Trying to decide what jewelry Mandy should wear with her gown. Let's go upstairs to your room."

Amanda knew her friend would use one pretext or another to get her alone, so she agreed to the first excuse, deciding it was better to get the discussion over with as soon as possible.

"Now, tell the truth, Amanda," Cheryl demanded as they mounted the stairs to her room. "Aren't you excited about meeting Jarod Colby?"

"No, I'm not. I haven't given that man a thought in over three years. He doesn't mean anything to me anymore." Amanda walked into her room and crossed over to sit on the blue gingham bedspread.

"I know that isn't true. Nobody ever forgets her first love, especially if he got away. You end up comparing every man you meet with him. Even if you married someone else, you'd always wonder what it would be like with that one special man."

"And how did you get to be such an authority?" Amanda teased, smoothing back her shoulder-length hair.

"It's common sense."

"Don't let Brad hear you talking that way!"

"Oh, Amanda, you of all people should know I've had a crush on your brother for years," the girl laughed, shaking the crop of dark curls on her head. "I imagine I'm speaking partly from experience."

"You can hardly compare Brad with Jarod Colby," Amanda replied dryly.

"Not as individuals," Cheryl agreed. "But mark my words, no one ever gets over her first love."

"Cheryl!" Mrs. Bennett's voice called from

downstairs. "Your mother's telephoned. She wants to know if you put the meat loaf in the oven."

"Tell her I'm on my way home now," Cheryl answered, making a face as she walked to the door. "I'll see you later, Mandy."

"Tobe wants Brad to call him tonight."

"Do you know—" Cheryl paused in the doorway "—my main competition for Brad's attention is Tobe Peterson. I could deal with another girl."

"I wouldn't worry about it," Amanda laughed.

But the laughter died when Cheryl disappeared from sight. Amanda walked over to the small dressing table, skirted with fabric to match her bedspread. Before it was a small bench covered in blue. Sitting on it, she stared into the oval mirror.

She was a mature woman now. There was no dreamy-eyed girl staring back at her anymore. She was twenty-one years old, an adult. Her face and figure were that of a woman retaining no blush of youth. Yet Amanda wondered if people ever did really grow up. Didn't some part of them always remain young and childlike?

Cinderella, Snow White, and Rapunzel all had their Prince Charmings. In the days and years of budding womanhood with all the fairy tales so fresh in her mind, Amanda had sought hers. It was simple. All you had to do was wish on a star, carry a lucky penny, and put a four-leafed clover in your locket. At fifteen, it had seemed possible.

Some of her friends had fallen in love with film stars or singing idols. Not Amanda. She was more realistic, she told herself. She had fallen in love with Jarod Colby.

Six years ago on a brisk November morning, she had been tramping through the woods, dreaming about love and romance and the handsome man she would one day meet—Prince Charmings are always handsome. That was when she had seen Jarod Colby for the first time. Prior to that day the members of the Colby family had been nebulous figures. She knew they existed, but they weren't really real.

Then Jarod Colby had cantered his horse across the meadow, passing not more than ten feet from where Amanda had stood in the shadow of the trees. The Colby insignia had been emblazoned on the saddle blanket or she might never have connected the dark rider with the family. He had ridden past her without seeing her, his gaze focused on some distant spot on the horizon.

Although she had watched him until he disappeared, she had only caught a fleeting glimpse of his face. Thick black hair had gleamed like a raven's wing, catching the sunlight as it fell in a tousled, rakish angle over his tanned forehead. His profile had revealed a straight nose and strong cheekbones and chin. Dressed all in black, he had been a very romantic figure.

Amanda had stayed in that spot for nearly three hours, hoping to see him again, but he didn't come back. It became imperative that she find out who he was. The only one who knew anything about the Colby company was her father. He had worked in their cotton mill since before he and her mother were married. Too shy to reveal the true reason she wanted to find out about the man on the horse, she had inquired about him once she was home on the pretext that the horse had been beautiful.

"That must have been Jarod Colby, the son," her father had answered. "He's the only one that rides. It seems such a waste of money to maintain the stables and horses when he's here only a few weeks out of the year."

"No one has ever accused the Colby family of not being extravagant," her mother had commented somewhat dryly. "Someone at church the other day remarked that Mr. and Mrs. Colby are going on another European tour right after Christmas. The way they're always flitting off somewhere it's a wonder that their company manages to keep its head above water."

"I met young Colby the other day." Her father had been puffing on his pipe and paused to tamp down the tobacco. Amanda had waited breathlessly for him to continue, unbearably eager to hear anything about the man she had seen. "He stopped in at the mill, something I don't ever recall his father doing. Usually all I see are the accountants. The boy struck me as being very astute."

"How old is he?" Amanda had murmured.

"Must be around twenty-six."

Then the subject had been changed. But Amanda's first love had been in the growing stages. The spot where she had first seen him had become almost holy ground. She would go there at every opportunity to relive the moment and wait for the time she would see him again; but the times she saw him were very few and always at a distance. His parents had been killed in an air crash and his visits to Georgia became increasingly less frequent.

One year went by, then two. The fantasies and dreams had dimmed somewhat, but they were always there in the background. Amanda dated, even went so far as to go steady with a boy, but he couldn't meet the ideal she had in her mind—Jarod Colby—and they broke up. In the spring of her seventeenth year she had decided to get a job as a tour guide in the plantation home owned by the Colbys—Oak Run. She never admitted it openly that she nurtured secret hopes of meeting Jarod Colby, yet it was there, tucked away in her subconscious. Someday he would meet her face to face and realize that he loved her.

The Colbys hadn't lived in Oak Run for more than thirty years. A rambling, ranch-style home had been built some distance from the plantation. It was called the Winter House by the local townspeople since the Colby family only occupied it during that season, and Amanda easily acquired a job as tour guide that summer. One afternoon Mrs. Matthews, who was Jarod's aunt, had sent her over the Winter House to pick up some brochures that had been left there by mistake.

Amanda had no more than parked the car in the driveway when Jarod Colby had come striding out of the house. Never would she forget how her heart had raced. This was her moment—or so she had thought as she had stepped eagerly out of the car.

"What are you doing here? Don't you know this is private property?" A black scowl had covered his face and he had glared at her, evincing none of the pleasure she had expected to see. Nor did his expression alter as she stood in numb silence, her throat frozen by the derisive look.

Not even when she was able to speak and could explain that she had a legitimate reason for being there did his attitude change. By the time she had retrieved the brochures and left, she was sick to her stomach. Jarod Colby in the flesh had turned out to be nothing like the Jarod Colby of her dreams—kind, solicitous, tender and romantic. And the humiliation she had suffered at that experience remained. The pain of his rejection, although it could hardly be called rejection, had lingered for months.

Blinking out of her reverie, Amanda turned from the mirror. When she had first heard his name downstairs, her reaction had been to the ideal she had made of him. Even though it still hurt a little to recall that day he had treated her so arrogantly, as though she was someone not worthy to walk on the same ground as he, it was better to remind herself that he was a hard, unfeeling brute. She was too old to be carried away by the fantasies of the past.

Perhaps, as her grandfather said, when she met him at the cotillion she would spit in his eye. And Amanda chuckled at the thought of his outraged reaction if she did.

CHAPTER TWO

A SET OF KNUCKLES rapped impatiently against her bedroom door. "Amanda, will you hurry up!" Brad muttered angrily. "You're holding up everything."

"She'll be there in just a minute," her mother answered for her. "Now, hold still, Amanda, so I can get this last pin in."

Obediently Amanda remained immobile, her brown eyes dancing with excitement as she watched her mother insert the rhinestone-studded hairpin into her hair. Red gold ringlets tickled the back of her neck while shimmering waves framed her face and accented the delicate ivory complexion. Her long, gold-tipped lashes hid the faint hint of green shadow on her eyelids, and a becoming shade of beige pink colored her lips.

"I'm as nervous as if I were going to my first dance," Amanda confided, slipping on the long pale green gloves her mother handed her.

"It's the social event of the year. You'll be rubbing elbows with the élite of the county," Mrs. Bennett said nodding, and stepping back to survey the completed product with a gleam of love in her eyes. "And they'll all be staring at you, saying 'Who is that beautiful redhead in green?'"

"Mom, you do wonders for a person's ego," Amanda laughed nervously. "I'd better go down," she declared, unnecessarily smoothing the sleek taffeta material of her gown. "If Tobe waits much longer, he's liable to back out and not take me at all."

The large hooped skirt of the gown gave the effect that Amanda was gliding down the stairs and across the living room to where her brother and Cheryl and Tobe were waiting.

"You are a bit overdressed for a pizza parlor," Tobe teased, producing a corsage that he had been holding behind his back.

"After all the work I put into that gown, Tobias Peterson, you'd better not take her anywhere else except to Oak Run!" her mother responded in mock anger.

"If we went anywhere else in these clothes, they'd put us in a loony bin," Tobe inserted, glancing at Amanda and smiling. "You look gorgeous. I might not mind getting locked up with you."

"Look on the bright side, Tobe," Brad spoke up. "Be grateful it's Jeff Davis's birthday we're celebrating and not George Washington's. The men wore wigs in his day."

"Both of you boys look very elegant in those suits," Mrs. Bennett stated.

"I don't know why they couldn't just have a dance," Tobe grumbled playfully. "Leave it to old lady Matthews to come up with the idea of wearing costumes of the pre–Civil War days!"

"I think it's fun," Cheryl declared. "Don't you, Amanda?"

"A woman certainly feels very feminine in these dresses," Amanda agreed, taking the corsage from Tobe and, with help from her mother, pinning it to the snug-fitting waistline of her gown. The pale, yellow green petals of the orchid were perfectly set off by the vivid green of the gown.

"I should have borrowed the truck," said Tobe.

"The truck? Whatever for?" Cheryl asked, tilting her head curiously in his direction.

"I don't know if you girls are going to be able to fit in my car," he replied impishly. "Those skirts will take up the whole seat."

"I think we can manage," Amanda grinned.

"I keep worrying that I'm going to forget about these hoops, sit down, and have the skirt fly up in my face," Cheryl murmured. "You're used to it, Amanda, having to wear these gowns all the time at Oak Run."

"They don't have many chairs at the cotillion except for the older ladies, for fear some woman will forget to adjust her hoops correctly when she sits down," Amanda explained.

"Do you mean we have to stand all night?" Brad moaned.

"When you aren't dancing with me," Cheryl replied pertly.

"All they do is waltz," he grumbled, then smiled at the petulant look on Cheryl's face. "That won't be so bad, I guess."

Cheryl turned a beaming smile on Tobe. "I don't know if I ever thanked you for arranging things so Brad and I could go to the cotillion, too."

"You didn't think I was going to go and be bored by myself, did you?" he chuckled, his blue gray eyes sparkling beneath a mockingly arched brow.

"If you stand there talking much longer," Amanda's father declared, walking into the living room with his pipe and a newspaper in his hand, tall and lanky like all his sons, "you're going to miss the dance altogether. You're already late."

"Nobody arrives on time, Mr. Bennett," Cheryl said grinning.

"Here, Amanda, take this with you. It might be a little cool tonight," her mother instructed, handing her a three-cornered shawl of the same material as her gown.

"Do you suppose we're late enough to leave now?" Brad teased.

"The sooner we go, the sooner we can leave," Tobe added, winking at Mrs. Bennett, who wore a pseudo expression of exasperation.

There was a chorus of goodbyes mingled with "enjoy yourselves" as the two couples made their way out of the house to Tobe's car. Her parents waved from the porch, standing the way Amanda always thought of them, with one of her father's long arms draped over the shoulder of his slightly plump wife. They were more than husband and wife. They were friends, and it was impossible to think of one without the other.

When they arrived at Oak Run, the two-and-a-half-story brick mansion was ablaze with lights shining from every window. Spotlights had been discreetly secreted among the ancient oaks and hidden in bushes edging the portico. Their light illuminated the six towering white columns, each five feet in diameter, that graced the front entrance of Oak Run.

"I feel like a pixie in grown-up clothes beside you," Cheryl declared in a nervous whisper as she and Amanda mounted the portico steps ahead of Tobe and Brad. "I should have worn a wig." Her hand self-consciously touched the short brunette curls that so artfully framed her angular face.

"You look lovely," Amanda insisted, glancing at the pink gown that emphasized the petite femininity of her friend.

"Remember that time we hid in the bushes to peep through the windows at the cotillion?" she whispered.

"And nearly got caught," Amanda reminded her.

The gleaming white-enameled double doors opened into the main hall, three times the size of the Bennetts' living room. A Y-shaped staircase dominated the hall, accented by a brass and crystal chandelier hanging above the center landing. Amanda noticed that the scrolled antique table had been removed from the hall, replaced by one less valuable, but the portrait of Colonel Colby still hung above it. Her poor grandfather would be enraged if he knew a painting of a Yankee soldier was displayed in this antebellum home.

A gentle melody from a string quartet floated through the open doors on the right where the ballroom was located. After the girls had passed their shawls to one of the several uniformed servants, the four moved toward the sound of the music. Cheryl still walked beside Amanda, her face filled with the bubbling excitement that consumed her. Amanda, too, caught the contagious feeling as they approached the ballroom.

They reached the doors to enter at the same moment as two men were going out, and a wave of giddiness washed over Amanda as she stared into Jarod Colby's face. All four stopped, including Tobe and Brad, who were walking behind the girls. Vitality radiated from the man in front of Amanda. His features were more firmly drawn, exhibiting no remaining softness of youth; his expression was cynically aloof almost to the point of harshness. The hair was still as ebony black as his eyes, and a masculine aura emanated from his tall, muscular frame. He was a rogue, flagrantly challenging a woman every second.

As her mind instantaneously registered all this, Amanda was aware of his gaze on her, sweeping over her gown and the nipped waistline, lingering for insolent seconds on the shadowy hollow of her breasts revealed by the gown. Then his unrevealing eyes moved to her face, again in obvious appraisal. The boldness of his cynical gaze made her feel stripped and naked. Light-headedly Amanda was conscious of pain in her left arm. It took her a moment to realize that Cheryl was gripping it so tightly no blood could flow through it.

"Ladies." Jarod Colby's low-pitched voice was accompanied by an imperious nod while he and the man with him, whom Amanda hadn't even looked at, moved aside to allow them to enter.

Her feet automatically carried her into the ball-room, although she wasn't aware of ordering them to do so. Through sheer force of will she calmed the wild fluctuations of her clamoring heart and resisted the impulse to turn to see if he was watching her.

"Did you see the way he looked at you?" Cheryl whispered. "I could have been King Kong for all the notice he took of me. I knew something like this was going to happen!"

"Nothing happened," Amanda said firmly, more to convince the romantic winging of her heart. "In five minutes he won't even remember he saw me."

"Honey, you were imprinted in his mind with indelible ink," Cheryl declared with a laugh.

At that moment Tobe moved forward to Amanda's side, preventing her from commenting on Cheryl's last remark. "You were right—there isn't a vacant chair anywhere."

A glance around the room with its polished oak woodwork and cream yellow walls indicated that the few chairs scattered around the edge were taken by the older participants in the celebration. To prevent her gaze from straying toward the door, Amanda directed it toward the French doors leading into the garden. The gold damask curtains were drawn back and flickering torchlights filtered through the white sheer insets on the doors. Only a dozen couples were gliding over the highly polished white floor, waltzing to the strains of the "Blue Danube." All the interior light came from two enormous crystal chandeliers, one at each end of the room.

A waiter was approaching them, carrying a tray of drinks. Cheryl touched her arm and leaned forward. "Are you supposed to drink with gloves on?" she murmured self-consciously.

"I think eating is the only thing that's taboo with gloves," Amanda replied.

"I'm so afraid I'm going to do some terribly gauche thing," Cheryl declared, pressing a hand against her stomach.

Amanda took two drinks from the tray and handed one to Cheryl. "Drink this," she ordered. "It might settle your nerves."

The truth was she felt in need of it herself. She had truly not believed that seeing Jarod Colby would affect her very much, and certainly not to the extent that it had. She was an adult, mentally and legally, and she wasn't about to allow a fantasy of the past to take possession of her again.

Taking a sip of her drink, Amanda ordered her mind to concentrate on the conversation between her brother and Tobe. Whether it was due to the strength of her determination not to allow her thoughts to dwell on Jarod Colby, or the fact that she didn't see him, nearly an hour later Amanda found she was enjoying herself, laughing and joking among her friends and meeting acquaintances of Tobe's family.

An attorney named Carl Grierson who had just joined them said to Tobe, "I haven't seen you dancing with this beautiful young lady tonight."

A twisted smile quirked one corner of Tobe's mouth. "This isn't the music I'm used to dancing to, and those skirts with their hoops don't allow a man to enjoy the advantages of dancing slowly with a girl."

Actually Tobe had danced with her once, exhibiting an expertise and fluidity of movement that had surprised Amanda. Yet he had seemed embarrassed by it, as if he wished that he possessed the stilted steps of her brother.

"With a lady as lovely as this one—" the attorney winked at her "—the honor is in being her partner. May I claim this dance?"

A nod from Tobe signaled his permission, and with a mock curtsy Amanda accepted the invitation. A faint smile of pleasure dimpled her cheeks as her partner led her to the dance floor. She enjoyed dancing to any kind of music, but the swishing material of her gown was made for the gracefully stately tunes of the past.

The middle-aged attorney was more than an adequate partner as he sedately guided her around the floor. The height of her heels put her nearly eye level with him, but at five foot five in her stockinged feet, she was hardly a dwarf.

"You dance as beautifully as you look," he commented. His head dipped slightly in salute, enabling her to see the reason his hair was combed forward—to conceal the rapidly receding hairline.

"You make it very easy for me," Amanda replied, feeling suddenly very much like a Southern belle, artfully turning compliments back on the giver.

"If you had a dance card and I were ten years younger, I would insist on claiming every dance with you. Unfortunately my wife might have some objections to that." He smiled, his pale blue eyes crinkling at the corners.

She tipped her head back and released the laughter that sprang so easily to her lips. But the movement changed her line of vision and Amanda found herself staring into the dark eyes of Jarod Colby. He was standing on the sidelines, ostensibly talking to a group of men, but his eyes were on her, retaining that same cool look of analytical appraisal as before. Nothing on his face revealed that he liked what he saw. There was no provocative gleam or message of appreciation in his gaze. Yet the very fact that he was watching her caused her heart to beat faster.

Forcing her gaze to slide nonchalantly from his, Amanda refocused on her partner. "You're very good for a girl's ego," she smiled.

"Believe me, it isn't difficult to compliment you. You're what I envisioned Scarlett O'Hara to look like, but with flaming red gold hair. Do you live here?"

The rest of the dance was occupied with questions and answers relating to Amanda's family. Her gaze didn't stray to Jarod Colby, although he managed to remain in her peripheral vision and she felt sure he was still watching her. There was a feeling of exultation in her heart that she couldn't ignore, no matter how much she tried to convince herself that his apparent interest in her didn't mean a thing.

But when Carl Grierson returned her to Tobe with a laughing comment that he was off to pacify his wife, she found it exceedingly difficult to forget Jarod Colby's presence in the room. All the arguments that he was an arrogant snob and tyrant, a man she heartily disliked because of his rudeness to her several years ago, faded into the background, and she found herself wondering if she hadn't condemned him too harshly because of one minor incident.

There was a stifled gasp from Cheryl in midsentence while she was pointing out a necklace worn by one of the guests. "He's coming this way!" Her voice was lowered to a squeaking whisper of excitement.

Amanda didn't need to turn around to find out who Cheryl meant. Without wasting a guess, she knew it would be Jarod Colby. The acrobatic movements of her stomach were at odds with her attempt to appear composed. As his tall form entered her side vision, she noted his unhurried approach, nodding or speaking to the other guests while he continued the progress that would bring him to their group.

When he was only two steps away from them, Amanda allowed her gaze to be drawn to him while permitting only a mild show of interest to be displayed. His eyes were on Tobe, ignoring the two girls completely, much to Amanda's chagrin.

Very smoothly, he extended a hand to Tobe. "Jarod Colby," he introduced himself. "You are John Peterson's son, aren't you?"

"Yes. Tobe Peterson," Tobe supplied. Then he turned to Brad, who was standing beside him. "This is my friend, Brad Bennett. His girl, Cheryl Weston. His sister and my date, Amanda Bennett."

A small part of her admired the way Tobe made the introductions with ease while she watched Jarod Colby shake hands with her brother, nodding politely and with equal interest to her and Cheryl in turn. She was too conscious of him standing between her and Tobe to pay attention to the polite conversation they were exchanging. Her senses were dominated by his potent virility and his ruggedly compelling features.

His lack of any display of interest in her during the first few minutes made it a surprise when she found herself looking into his jet black eyes. "With your escort's permission, I would like to have this dance with you," he stated, his tone implying that he expected no opposition from her or Tobe.

"I have no objection," Tobe murmured, a curious smile on his face when he looked at Amanda.

On general principles she should refuse, she thought, then chided herself for dwelling on some imagined hurt of the past. After all, he was only asking her to dance, she told herself, just as she heard the bandleader announce that it would be a "change partners" dance. Idly she wondered if Jarod had known that when he asked her and decided that he had.

"I would be delighted, Mr. Colby," she answered coolly, offering him her hand.

She felt his eyes move lazily over the erect carriage of her head, which she kept averted. There was a satirically amused gleam in his eyes when he turned her into his arms on the dance floor. For lingering seconds he held her eyes with the compelling blackness of his gaze before he began to move her in time to the song. The firm pressure of his hand on her back left her in no doubt as to who was leading whom.

"Amanda—a soft gentle name with a hint of spirit," he commented. "Yet it fits the languid, drawling speech of the South."

"That's true," Amanda replied with a nod, prickling a little as she wondered if she had heard a hint of mockery in his voice. "And you Yankees always seem to have such hard, uncompromising names, like Jarod."

"The way you say it, it doesn't sound hard at all." The lines deepened around his mouth without humor and she knew he hadn't missed the bite in her voice. "Do you live here in Oak Springs?"

"All my life," she answered, gazing past the expensive black material of his suit and the silver gray waistcoat accenting the muscular chest.

"It's strange that we've never met."

"Oh, but we have." Her lips tightened fractionally as she remembered the blow her ego had suffered at his hands.

"When was that?" His eyes were making a relentless search of her face as though he was seeking something that would be familiar.

"About four or five years ago when I first came to work here at Oak Run," she answered, discovering a candor she didn't know she possessed. "I was sent over to the Winter House for some brochures by your aunt, and you very peremptorily ordered me off your property."

"I'm ashamed to say I don't remember meeting

you." But he didn't look ashamed and made no effort to apologize for his actions. "Did you get your brochures?"

"Yes, after you'd stopped insulting me long enough to hear my explanation for why I was there."

His eyes were guardedly thoughtful as they met the slightly defiant look of hers. "You must have formed a very bad opinion of me."

"Yes." Her answer was simple and direct.

"Then I must persuade you to change your opinion." A smile glinted in his eyes, although the line of his mouth didn't alter.

The pressure of his hand against the back of her waist increased as he whirled her into a fast series of spins while keeping to the gliding tempo of the melody. Her eyes saw the dancers separating and seeking new partners and Amanda realized the signal to change must have been given.

"We're supposed to change partners now," she informed him.

This time there was a decidedly mocking tilt of his head. "One of the advantages of being Jarod Colby of Colby Enterprises is doing what I want to do."

"Yes, but—" she began, seeing the interested glances from the others at their failure to change partners.

"I thought you wanted to dance with me," Jarod chided.

"I do." Then she wished she hadn't replied so quickly.

"It shouldn't bother you to discover everyone is

watching us," he murmured, holding her gaze again while he made another cool appraisal of her attributes—an action that wasn't complimentary but rather assessing, as if he was deciding if she was worthy of his interest. "There are quite a few men who haven't been able to take their eyes off you this evening. The combination of that gown and your hair would capture any man's attention, and the fact that you have a face and figure to complement them increases his interest."

"You're very flattering." Amanda swallowed nervously, trying to conceal the fact that he had the ability to disturb as well as antagonize her. "But people are looking at me now because I'm dancing with you."

"Not just because you're dancing with me," he corrected smoothly, "But because I don't intend to relinquish my possession of you. You might as well know that I'm accustomed to getting what I want, Amanda."

She wasn't sure how much she was supposed to read into that statement. That he wanted to dance with her was obvious, but was he implying more than that? Many times she had imagined herself in a similar situation with this very man. Now she found he was an unknown quantity that she didn't know how to handle.

When she continued to remain silent, he said, "Are you afraid to ask what I want?" His deep, husky voice vibrated over her.

"You've already told me," she replied, trying to force a lightness into the charged atmosphere. "You want me to revise my opinion."

There was another signal to change partners which Jarod ignored. "And I shall succeed in doing that."

It rankled that he was so certain of his attraction. "Will you?" Amanda challenged, haughtily arching a red brown eyebrow.

"I must have already partially succeeded. You're dancing with me."

"I had the impression I was ordered to dance with you." Attraction shifted to antagonism. "I didn't think it was permissible to ignore a royal summons."

The amused glint in his eyes told her that he didn't believe one word she was saying. "I believe it was a case of knowing that I was attracted to you and it would give you a chance to score off on me for that incident a long time ago. And perhaps a little bit of curiosity."

Attracted to her! The words struck at her midriff like a physical blow. There was no longer any need to try to surmise his reasons for being with her. It was out in the open, plainly stated that he was attracted to her. In spite of all her efforts to remain poised, inside Amanda was quivering like a schoolgirl. Her legs were incredibly weak and it was with relief that she discovered the last note of the song was fading away. She needed time to compose herself and regain the perspective of Jarod Colby the man, instead of Jarod Colby the dream.

When their steps ended, the hand on her waist claimed her elbow, gently guiding her off the dance floor. Her gaze quickly sought the side of the room where Cheryl, Brad, and Tobe had been standing, only they weren't there.

"Would you care for some refreshment?" Jarod asked.

The small buffet table was in front of them, a punch bowl filled with shimmering red liquid and surrounded by ornate cut-glass cups. Platters of artistically prepared hors d'oeuvres flanked the sides of the bowl.

"Some punch, please," Amanda requested, her eyes straying around the room for some sign of her friends.

In what seemed like mere seconds, he was holding a cup in front of her, his gaze noting her search of the room. She took the cup from him and held it nervously in both hands.

"Would you like something to eat?"

"No," Amanda refused politely, her glance straying to the bite-size morsels on the platters, then returning to her gloved hands.

"I forgot," Jarod murmured, arching a thick brow in her direction. "It isn't proper to eat with gloves on, is it? We can remedy that." She watched him curiously as he eyed the trays, wondering if he intended removing her gloves. "This pâté looks very tasty." He picked it up and turned to Amanda. "Open wide."

Self-consciously she drew back as she realized he intended to place it in her mouth. Her action brought another glitter of amusement into the obsidian black eyes. She had the feeling he was going to hold it inches in front of her mouth until she gave in, and the longer she hesitated, the more likely someone would see them. Unwillingly Amanda opened her mouth. His fingers brushed her lips as he placed it in her mouth. The sensation of his touch remained, the incredibly intimate contact changing her blood into liquid wildfire.

"Your friends seem to have deserted you," Jarod murmured after Amanda had managed to swallow the hors d'oeuvre.

"I don't know where they could have gone," she answered, her gaze anxiously searching the room again.

"Perhaps they've stepped out on the veranda for a breath of air," he suggested.

"Yes, they may have."

"Shall we go look for them?"

CHAPTER THREE

AMANDA HESITATED, feeling ridiculously awkward and out of her depth. She felt uncomfortable standing beside Jarod in a room full of people, and to be alone with him on the veranda would disturb her even more. Still, she had to find Tobe and the rest. Thankfully she was aware that none of her inner agitation was revealed in her expression as she accepted his suggestion.

There were several knowing looks cast their way as she and Jarod walked through the French doors onto the veranda outside. Very few people were outdoors. Mostly they were men who had come out to smoke cigars or cigarettes. Amanda was conscious of Jarod lighting a cigarette while she tried to peer through the shadows cast by the flickering torchlights.

"Are you going to college or working?" Jarod was the first to break the silence as his hand once more closed over her elbow and began guiding her along the darkened path into the garden walk extending out from the veranda.

"Both," she answered, catching a glimpse of three figures standing beneath an oak tree and holding her breath, only to discover that all three were men. "This fall will be the start of my last year in college."

"What are you studying?"

"English Literature with a minor in Journalism."

"Where are you working?"

"Here at Oak Run. I'm still a tour guide," she answered with an expressive lift of her shoulders.

"No wonder you look so natural in that gown. You wear them all the time." His steps ceased and the pressure of his fingers on her arm forced her to do likewise. "If you're an example of the guides here, I'm going to have to take more notice of the people in my employ!"

Before Amanda realized what she was doing, she found herself thinking of the other girls who worked at Oak Run and which ones might appeal to Jarod, all the while fighting a twinge of jealousy.

"Looks are one of the requirements for the job," she managed to say.

"You're very beautiful."

His superior height put her at a disadvantage. The play of his gaze over her face and shoulders made her disturbingly aware of their solitude.

"Thank you," she breathed. Her mind was blank of any witty repartee to parry his compliment. She made a half turn to escape his eyes.

The night was languid and still. There was a roof of stars above the thick foliage of the giant oaks. Distantly the strains of a waltz filtered out of the plantation into the night air, while crickets chirped loudly in competition.

His fingers touched her neck and blazed a trail to her shoulders. "Your skin is very creamy." It was more of a comment than a compliment, yet it brought about the same reaction to her jumbled nerves.

Amanda turned back toward him, hoping to elude the touch of his hand gracefully. "Did you know crickets chirp until they...fi...find their mate?" What began as a bright attempt to change the conversation ended in a breathless whisper as his fingers moved down her shoulders, following the neckline of her dress over the swell of her breasts up to the opposite shoulder.

"No, I didn't know that," Jarod remarked dryly. His eyes, dark and unreadable, held hers, making her look into his while his fingers caressed the hollow of her throat. "I want to take you home." The suddenness of his statement jolted through her.

"It's impossible," she replied without any conviction in her voice.

"Nothing is impossible." A smile played with his lips.

"I've always made it a rule to leave a party with the man who brought me," Amanda said more positively.

"Rules are made to be broken." His gaze strayed to her mouth, which she had nervously moistened.

"Would you feel the same way if you'd been the one to bring me?" she asked, resisting the almost overwhelming temptation to agree.

The corners of his mouth turned up in a humorless smile. "If you were my date, I wouldn't have brought you to this charade. I would have taken you to a place where we could be alone."

"Well, that doesn't happen to be the case, since I did come here with Tobe," Amanda stated. "It's only proper that I leave with him. As a matter of fact—" she swallowed, fighting the chill that shivered over her skin as his hand fell back to his side "—he must be wondering where I've gone."

"Maybe by now he's back inside," Jarod suggested.

He didn't look the least bit disappointed that he hadn't been able to change her mind. Ironically Amanda was the one who felt disappointed that he hadn't persisted, but she successfully hid it as they retraced their steps through the garden and into the ballroom. Brad, Cheryl, and Tobe were waiting just inside, and with a nod Jarod left her with them.

Amanda was convinced that she had seen the last of Jarod Colby. The instant he had left her, she saw him walk over to an attractive blonde and escort her onto the dance floor. She scolded herself for feeling so let down. He had only been flirting with her, more than likely expecting her to fall at his feet because he deigned to pay attention to her. But those moments she had been with him, subjected to his unmistakable magnetism, had left a vivid impression.

Unwillingly she had to admit that it hurt to watch him dancing with another girl, knowing he was probably saying the same things to her. When Tobe asked her to dance, she accepted eagerly, determined to show Jarod Colby that his absence didn't bother her at all.

"What did you think of the local lord?" Tobe asked.

"A bit too arrogant," she answered with a shrug, keeping the brittle smile in place.

"He knows what he wants and he usually gets it. Has he decided he wants you?"

"I'm a little country girl. I think his taste runs more to sophisticated blondes." Amanda knew Tobe had seen Jarod dancing with the girl and her pride insisted that she be the first one to comment on it. "I expect he's a tyrant to work for."

"You and your father work for him—indirectly, at least," Tobe reminded her. "He's a very intelligent and astute businessman, unlike his father, who was more interested in spending money than making it."

Amanda didn't want to hear about the supposedly good qualities of Jarod Colby. Right now she needed to banish him from her mind, if that was possible. She was not going to allow her mind to build another totally false picture of the man, as she had done before.

"When are your parents coming back?" she asked, changing the subject.

"Who cares?" he answered, grimacing.

"Tobe, you don't really feel that way," she scolded, the way her mother always did.

He sighed heavily. "I don't think any of you Bennetts realize how lucky you are. Your parents are always there when you need them. I remember when my dog was killed by a car on the highway. I was about nine at the time and ran crying home to my father. He gave me the money to buy another dog. It was your dad who went out there with me and got the body. He was the one who built the box and dug the hole so we could bury him." There was a savage shake of his head. "If I had my way, I'd never go home again. I think it's your mother who makes me. The Bennetts are my family."

"We feel as if you're a part of us, too," Amanda murmured softly, for the first time realizing there was such a thing as a poor rich kid.

But Tobe was never one to feel sorry for himself for long. In fact, he did it rarely. "Let's change to a more pleasant subject," he suggested, winking down at her.

At that moment a hand tapped the back of Tobe's shoulder and a voice said, "Shall we change partners?"

Both Tobe and Amanda glanced in surprise at the couple dancing beside them. It was Jarod and the blonde. Amanda's feet wouldn't move and Tobe interpreted her halting as agreement to change. Not until Jarod's arm circled her waist did her heart start beating again, then at a rapid pace. Her brown eyes searched the unfathomable expression on his face.

"Did you think you'd seen the last of me?" Jarod mocked softly.

His astute perception brought a flush of rare color to her cheeks. Amanda glanced at the attractive blonde now openly flirting with Tobe.

"She's very attractive," she murmured.

"I believe your date thinks so," Jarod replied complacently. "Many men find my cousin attractive."

"Your cousin?" she repeated, casting a startled glance at his face. The amusement written there told her he had guessed that she hadn't known the girl.

"Judith will keep him occupied for the rest of the evening," he stated, "and that should eliminate your objections to my taking you home."

"No." There was an infinitesimal shake of her head. "No, I won't go home with you."

His fingers tightened cruelly around her gloved hand. "Don't play games!" he muttered. "You said earlier that you couldn't let me take you home because of your date. He's out of the picture now."

"How can you be so sure?" Amanda protested.

A bitter sound like laughter came from his mouth. "Because I control the family purse strings and Judith needs money." His eyes narrowed, sweeping over her face in open possession. "Do you want me to take you home or not? A simple yes or no is all I want."

Pain jabbed at her stomach. It would be so easy to say yes, to be swept along by the magnetism that surrounded him. Yet Amanda was just as conscious that he was treating her with the same arrogance and superiority he had exhibited those many years ago when he had ordered her off his property.

She raised her chin slightly. "The answer is no, Mr. Colby," she said firmly.

A dark brow arched momentarily, reflecting his surprise at her answer. Amanda guessed the occasions were rare when he didn't get his way, especially with women.

"I see," Jarod murmured coldly.

"I doubt very much that you do." The chill in her voice surprised even her. "I don't think other people's principles have ever mattered very much to you." The music ended and they stood facing one another. "I do hope your cousin receives her money. It was not her fault that you didn't succeed in your objective. Good evening, Mr. Colby." The whirl of her skirt signaled her departure as she left him standing alone.

Tobe was on the opposite side of the dance floor talking to the blond Judith. Amanda sent her brother over to get him, pleading a headache as the reason she wanted to leave. The excuse didn't fool Cheryl, but she guessed Amanda had a valid reason and didn't question her.

A GIRL DRESSED in an old-fashioned organdy gown of lavender and a large floppy hat came scurrying toward Amanda. "People are standing outside waiting to go on the tour," she declared worriedly. "They're getting impatient. "We were supposed to open up fifteen minutes ago."

"I realize that, Pam," Amanda answered calmly. "The cleaning crew are finishing now. It will only be a few minutes more."

"With the cotillion last night, they should have closed this place today," the girl grumbled. "Or else they should have had the cleaning crew come in earlier."

"Unfortunately there wasn't anyone here to let them in earlier, but that's not our concern." Amanda's own temper was reaching boiling point, but she forced herself to stay cool. "Has Susan arrived yet?"

"She called," the girl named Pam answered, adding sarcastically, "She claimed her car wouldn't start. More than likely she overslept. She said she'd be here in an hour."

"All right," Amanda sighed, massaging the spot above her eyebrow that was throbbing with pain. "I'll take her tour through the first floor of the house. You'll guide them through the second floor and Linda will show them the gardens." She glanced around. "Where's Linda?"

On cue, the girl in question came hurrying into the hall, her pale pink gown identical to the ones Pam and Amanda were wearing, except for the color.

"The cleaning people have finished," she said breathlessly. "Shall I open the doors now?"

"Yes." Amanda nodded, smoothing the ruffles of her mint green dress. "And be sure to explain to them the reason for the delay. They're more than likely tourists and would have no knowledge of the cotillion that was held here last night. And I doubt that they would know it was Jefferson Davis's birthday yesterday."

Except for a few grumbles, the visitors to the plantation took the delay in good spirits. Amanda was glad she was the one taking them through the first part of the tour. She had more experience than the other girls and was able to keep them entertained with amusing anecdotes connected with the house. Once she was able to coax a smile or a glimmer of interest from all of them, she knew they would forget that they had had to wait.

As the group walked down a side hallway, one of the women asked, "How did the South acquire the name of Dixie? Was it taken from the Mason-Dixon Line?"

"No. The Mason-Dixon Line marked the boundaries between the states of Maryland and Pennsylvania, although it was eventually regarded as the demarcation line of the North and the South," Amanda explained. "The name Dixie originated in Louisiana, which was settled predominately by the French. Before the Civil War, a ten-dollar banknote was issued by the State of Louisiana with the French word for ten, which is spelled d-i-x, pronounced deese, printed on it. Americans pronounced it as dix and later referred to Louisiana as the land of the dixie, the place where such money was found. Gradually the term was applied to all of the South.

"This last room," Amanda said as she led the visitors into the large study with its rich pecan woodwork, "was where the running of the plantation took place. When the Union army commandeered the house during the Civil War, this room served as the private office of Colonel Bartholomew Colby. His staff was quartered here in the house and the rest of the company bivouacked in the grounds."

"What did they do with the owners of the plant-ation?" one of the women asked.

"At that time, only Mrs. Reagan and her daugh-ter were here. Her husband, Sean Reagan, was a cavalry officer under Robert E. Lee," Amanda ex-plained. "Colonel Colby allowed Mrs. Reagan and her daughter to occupy the master bedroom upstairs."

"How long were the colonel and his men here?" another man inquired.

"Only a few weeks. General Sherman had given orders that no private homes were to be de-stroyed during his march to the sea after the city of Atlanta was burned to the ground. It was an order that was eventually ignored, bringing about the destruction of almost all of the beautiful plantations that lay in the path of his march, which was some eighty miles wide at various points. However, Colonel Colby evidently appreciated the extraordinary beauty and grandeur of Oak Run and refused to let his soldiers put it to the torch."

"I don't believe that was his reason."

The voice came from the back of the room. Everyone, including Amanda, turned toward the speaker. Her composure was shaken as she saw Jarod Colby make his way slowly through the small group. His bland gaze was focused on her, causing her breath to come in uneven spurts.

"Ladies and gentlemen," she said, turning her attention from his with difficulty and forcing a bright smile to appear on her face, "this is a rare treat. I'd like you to meet Jarod Colby, a direct descendant of Colonel Colby and the present owner of Oak Run.''

There was a gracious nod of his black head at the scattering of applause and the buzz of whispered conversations. ''I do hope you're enjoying your tour,'' he said, turning to stand beside Amanda.

A man's voice raised itself above the various assertions that they were all enjoying the tour. ''You were about to tell us why the colonel didn't allow his men to burn the plantation.''

''I have no doubt that the colonel found this home very beautiful, as Miss Bennett pointed out,'' Jarod replied. ''But the true reason he left it standing was the same one that led him to purchase it after the war was over. He was infatuated with Mrs. Reagan.'' His dark gaze slid down to Amanda, dwelling briefly on the startled roundness of her eyes. ''You might call it the family secret. At the time that the Union troops occupied the house, Mrs. Reagan had been told that her husband was missing and presumed dead. As far as my ancestor was concerned, she was a widow. When the war ended and the prisoners were released, Mrs. Reagan and Colonel Colby discovered that her husband was very much alive, but an invalid. To persuade Sean Reagan to divorce his wife, the colonel paid him twice what the plantation was worth in its day. But Mrs. Reagan had a last-minute attack of conscience and refused to leave her husband, and there was no divorce. The colonel was left with the plantation and his lady fair left with the money and her husband.''

An uncomfortable hush settled over the small group. They followed Amanda a little slowly as she led them into the main hall where Pamela would take them through the second floor. Jarod was standing in the doorway of the study, obviously waiting for her when she had seen the last of the group follow Pam up the Y-shaped staircase.

"May I have a few minutes of your time, Miss Bennett?" Jarod asked mockingly. When Amanda looked hesitantly toward the front where a new group of tourists was gathering, he reached in his pocket and took out a stub. "The young lady wouldn't allow me in without purchasing a ticket, so I believe that allows me a few minutes to speak to you."

"You've never been here before, Mr. Colby, and the girl is new. It's understandable that she didn't know who you were, especially if you didn't identify yourself," Amanda replied with cool dignity.

"I'm sorry I'm late, Amanda." A girl came rushing up behind her. "The darned car wouldn't start." She glanced curiously at Jarod, and Amanda wondered how much Susan had heard before she joined them. "Do you want me to take the next tour on the first floor?"

"Yes," she nodded. "There's a group at the front ready to leave now."

"Okay," Susan agreed smiling. "It won't happen again—my being late, I mean."

"Now may I see you?" Jarod repeated as the other girl walked hurriedly to the front of the hall.

"I really don't know what we have to discuss," Amanda murmured.

"My aunt uses the old cloakroom as an office, I believe." Before she could protest, he was taking her by the arm and leading her there.

Once inside, Jarod closed the door behind them and leaned against it as if he expected Amanda to try to leave. He folded his arms in front of him and stared at her, and she shifted uncomfortably. The room seemed much smaller somehow.

"What did you want to talk to me about?" Amanda swallowed nervously and attempted to appear indifferent when she looked at him. He was wearing a summer suit of light gray that made him look taller and much more formidable with his jet dark looks.

"I want you to have dinner with me." The expression on his face was completely unreadable.

"When?" she queried, trying not to let him guess that his question had taken her by surprise.

"Tonight."

"That's very short notice." Her stomach was doing somersaults. Last night she had told herself that if Jarod was truly interested in her he would have asked her out. Now he was doing that very thing.

"Do you have other plans?" Jarod demanded, straightening away from the door.

"If I did, I imagine you would ask me to break them," Amanda retorted, more sharply than she intended.

"Then you are free tonight." He seized on her implication.

"Which doesn't necessarily mean I accept," she

retorted, tilting her chin at a defiant angle as she met his complacent gaze.

"What's bothering you?" Amusement lurked in his eyes. "Are you offended that the notice is so short?"

"Should I be grateful that you can fit me into your schedule?" she demanded. The muscles in her throat constricted painfully.

He chuckled softly and moved across the small room to take her by the shoulders. There was a fiery warmth in his eyes as they swept over her face. His expression became serious and compelling.

"The truth is I have to fly to Pennsylvania tomorrow morning. I won't be back until the end of the week," Jarod murmured, his husky voice caressing her with its velvet softness. "If it will soothe your injured pride, I'll ask you to keep next Saturday open, too." His thumbs were sensually rubbing her shoulders in a circular motion. "But come with me tonight. I don't want to wait an entire week before I see you."

The declaration took her breath away. She could only gaze at him in disbelief, her heart hammering against her ribs while a shimmery film of happiness sparkled in her brown eyes.

"Really?" It was a barely audible whisper that begged for his confirmation.

Jarod stood motionless, his hands stopping their caressive movement as he stared into her eyes. His own perceptibility darkened when his gaze moved to her trembling lips.

"I want to see you tonight." The urgency that vibrated in his voice transmitted itself to her.

"I'll be through here at six," Amanda said breathlessly. "I can be ready by seven—seven-thirty at the latest."

"I'll send a car for you."

"A car?" There was confusion in the look she gave him. "Aren't you coming to pick me up?"

Jarod smiled, and it was the first time she had noticed a smile reaching his eyes. Usually it was an impersonal movement of his mouth.

"Doesn't that meet with your approval, either?" he asked.

"It's all right," Amanda assured him quickly. "It's just that my parents...well, they're used to meeting my dates. Not that they would object if they didn't. It's simply something that I've always done."

"I'll be there at quarter-past seven. How's that?"

Her red gold hair was loose, lying in soft curls around her shoulders. Jarod twined a lock around his fingers, studied it for a moment, then brought his gaze to her face for an answer.

"Fine." Amanda gulped silently, wondering where the adult in her had fled.

"Seven-fifteen, you'll be ready?" He seemed to breathe in deeply as the words hovered in the air, half command and half question.

"Yes."

His gaze raked her face and shoulders one last time, then Jarod turned and left the room while Amanda remained where she stood. She resisted the impulse to pinch herself to make certain she wasn't dreaming and gave herself a mental shake.

She had to stop reacting to him with that childish infatuation she had once possessed. At the moment she was so confused that she didn't know if it was his potent attraction that was drawing her, or an image of the past. She had to stop confusing the two.

CHAPTER FOUR

THE REST OF THE DAY continued at the same frantic pace of the morning. The sunny June day had brought scores of people parading through Oak Run. It was half-past six before the last visitors left the grounds and Amanda could go home.

"You're late, dear," her mother commented as Amanda walked in the door.

"You wouldn't believe the chaos today," Amanda declared, turning her back to her mother so she could begin unhooking her dress. "Where is everybody?"

"Your father and brothers went fishing. There's cold chicken and potato salad in the refrigerator. You can help yourself."

"I'm going out to dinner and I only have about a half an hour to get ready," Amanda replied, holding the gown up with one hand as she started to hurry down the hallway to the stairs.

"You didn't mention that this morning." Her mother followed more sedately.

"I didn't know this morning," Amanda tossed over her shoulder. "Be a dear, mom, and draw me some bathwater while I lay out my clothes."

"Who is it that has you in such a dither?"

"I'm not in a dither. I'm just late," she protested. She held the long folds of her gown in her hand as she mounted the stairs. Self-consciously Amanda added, "Jarod Colby asked me out."

"Jarod Colby? *The* Jarod Colby?" Amanda's reply had stopped Mrs. Bennett halfway up the steps.

"What about Jarod Colby?" Her younger sister, Bonnie, appeared in the doorway of her bedroom.

"I'm going out with him tonight," Amanda answered, trying to make it sound like the most natural thing in the world while her heart beat a steady tattoo against her rib cage.

"You're kidding!" Bonnie squealed.

"I didn't know you even knew him." Her mother had regained control after her initial start of surprise.

"I met him at the cotillion last night and he stopped at Oak Run this morning to ask me out." Inside her room, Amanda stepped quickly out of her gown and began rummaging through her closet.

"Tonight? Isn't that rather short notice?" her mother murmured, a frown drawing her eyebrows together.

"I think it's terrific!" Bonnie sighed as she sunk onto the blue gingham spread covering Amanda's bed. "He meets you one night and the next day he comes looking for you because he can't get you out of his mind." Bonnie turned excitedly to her sister, her short auburn hair bouncing around her face. "What are you going to wear?"

"This black dress, I think," Amanda answered.

It was cut on classically simple lines with a snug-fitting bodice flaring out to an A-line skirt. Only narrow strips of material crossed her shoulders.

"You look so sophisticated in that!" Bonnie agreed enthusiastically.

"It is summer, though...." Amanda hesitated, looking back into her closet. "What do you think, mom?"

"Black is never wrong," was her mother's answer. "What time will he be here?"

"Seven-fifteen."

"I'd better get that bathwater started," Mrs. Bennett declared.

By some miracle Amanda was walking down the stairs when she heard the car pulling up out front. Bonnie had been keeping a vigil at the kitchen window and she came racing into the hallway.

"He's here, Mandy!" She tried to suppress the excitement in her voice and her words came out in a stifled shriek. "He's simply gorgeous!"

"Who's here? Who's gorgeous?" Her grandfather came shuffling from the living room. "Where are you going?"

"I have a date tonight," Amanda answered, deliberately ignoring his first questions. She brushed a kiss across the old man's face as the doorbell sounded. "I'll get it, mom," she called.

"So she has a date. What's all the fuss about?" her grandfather demanded as his daughter-in-law walked into the hall.

Their voices followed Amanda as she hurried toward the front door. Her heart seemed to be in her throat at the knowledge that Jarod Colby was standing on the other side.

"Her date is Jarod Colby," Bonnie informed her grandfather. "My sister is going out with Jarod Colby."

"Jarod Colby," he repeated. "And you are allowing her to go, Bernice!"

Amanda heard her mother's attempt to shush her grandfather as she opened the door. She stared into the strikingly masculine face with its chiseled features while his gaze moved over her.

"Hello," Jarod said quietly.

"Come in." Amanda moved back, suddenly overcome by a shyness that was completely unnatural to her.

With embarrassing clarity, her grandfather's gruff voice pierced the air. "Do you mean to tell me that you're allowing Mandy to go out with that carpetbagging northern Yankee?"

"Keep your voice down!" her mother admonished.

Amanda glanced apologetically at Jarod, but he only appeared amused by the outburst. "My grandfather," she explained quietly. "The Civil War ended only a few years ago as far as he's concerned."

"That's all right, I understand," Jarod replied.

Her mother moved swiftly towards them, her cheeks tinged with scarlet color. Her hand was extended in greeting to Jarod, which he accepted.

"I must apologize for my father-in-law's rudeness, Mr. Colby," her mother said quietly. "Discretion has never been one of his virtues."

"An apology isn't necessary," said Jarod, bestowing a rare smile on her mother. "I've been called worse things than a Yankee carpetbagger."

Her grandfather was still mumbling in the distance and Amanda turned to her mother. "We'll leave now," she said. "Don't wait up for me."

"Have a good time," Mrs. Bennett called after them as Amanda and Jarod walked through the door onto the porch.

"Is your father averse to Yankees, too?" Jarod asked, his dark eyes twinkling with laughter as he helped her into the car.

"No, thank heaven," Amanda smiled. "He's off fishing with my brothers."

"You have more than one brother?" The politeness of the question was overridden by the dark look he flashed at her, which seemed to say he was interested in anything that had to do with her.

"Actually there are six of us Bennett children. My oldest sister, Marybeth, is married with two lovely daughters. She and her husband live in Athens—Athens, Georgia, that is. Brian is a medical student, so he isn't home now. Teddy is studying law and Brad, the one you met last night, is going to be an architect. The baby of the family is my sister Bonnie. Thank goodness she's still in high school."

"Why do you say 'thank goodness'?"

"It's a strain on my parents' budget to have four of their children in college. Strain is probably an understatement," Amanda smiled. "We all work to help the kitty, but the brunt of the tuition costs are met by mom and dad.''

"What are you going to do when you graduate?'' A brow arched satirically. "Get married?''

"Not right away. I suppose I'll teach for a few years to pay back my parents' investment in me.'' The subject of marriage was not something she wanted to discuss, not when he gave the impression that he was listening to every nuance in her voice.

"You could marry a wealthy man and not have to worry about it,'' Jarod suggested dryly. His leg brushed her thigh as he slowed the car down to make a turn.

Her pulse pitter-pattered along her neck as she let her gaze sweep out the window. "I suppose I could,'' she murmured noncommittally. She didn't want him to think she was after him, although the prospect of having his arm around her was an increasingly irresistible thought. "But I'm not a mercenary person. Having money isn't among my list of priorities in life.''

He glanced at her thoughtfully and with a look of skepticism in the dark eyes. Amanda could understand why. He had probably met many people whose only interest in him was his money.

"It's a lovely evening,'' she sighed, glancing back to the view beyond the windshield.

"Yes, I thought we'd have dinner on the veranda.''

"The Veranda?'' she repeated. "Is that a new restaurant? Being away at the college most of the year, I'm not too familiar with all the new places.''

A soft chuckle rolled from his parted lips. "I told you last night that I would take you somewhere where we could be alone." His gaze physically caressed her before it turned back to the road. "I was speaking about the veranda at my house, not a restaurant."

"Oh," in a very small voice.

"Do you still want to have dinner with me?" Jarod challenged mockingly.

Her hands were folded in her lap, feeling suddenly clammy and cold. At the same time, she felt hot and light-headed. It had never occurred to her that he would be taking her to the Winter House. If she refused to go, she would seem very juvenile and prim. But the idea of sharing an intimate dinner with him, alone in his house, was a bit frightening. Then she chided herself for being so foolish. He wasn't the type to force himself on a woman.

The smile she gave him was bright and confident, not exactly a true reflection of the way she was feeling inside. "I do hope you have a good cook. I'm ravenous!"

His gaze slid over her, lingering for brief seconds on her mouth. "So am I," Jarod agreed. The wry note in his voice made Amanda believe that he wasn't talking about food, and the air in the car became very stifling.

"THAT WAS DELICIOUS," Amanda sighed, leaning determinedly back in her chair. "I do love strawberries."

"And whipped cream," Jarod added as he exhaled a puff of smoke from his cigarette and watched it swirl in front of him. "I always thought Southern girls ate before going out so their dates would think they had very small appetites."

"That was true in the olden days, but not anymore," she said with a smile.

"You can clear everything away, Hannah," he told the older woman as she walked through the open door into the screened extension of the house. "I won't need anything else tonight."

Not wanting to interfere with the housekeeper's work, Amanda rose from the table and wandered idly to the mesh wall, aware that Jarod was following her. The sun had dipped below the horizon, leaving a residue of shimmering golds and pinks behind.

A billow of smoke blew over her shoulder through the mesh screen into the coming night and she knew Jarod was standing behind her. The scent of tobacco and intoxicating masculine cologne seemed to wrap around her as she heard the housekeeper wheeling the serving trolley with the remains of their dishes out of the veranda.

She was suddenly very conscious of the fact that they were alone. He had dismissed the housekeeper for the evening and already explained that his aunt now lived in a small house in Oak Springs. With the sun down, it seemed to grow darker with each passing second. There was a need for movement, so Amanda turned and found herself staring into his face, dark and unfathomable. The corners of her mouth turned into a faint smile as she found she couldn't think of anything to say.

"It's growing dark. Would you like to go inside?" he asked, a hint of mockery vibrating in his voice.

"Yes," Amanda agreed hesitantly as he stepped to one side.

The screened patio led into the living room. A single light was on, sending a streamer of white across the floor. It was a large, masculine room, done in warm oranges and browns with a splattering of yellow gold for color.

"Would you like some music?" Jarod had walked over to an expensive stereo set before glancing over his shoulder to ask.

"Yes."

Immediately a soft, languid melody permeated the room through concealed speakers. Unsure of where she should sit, Amanda tried to appear interested in a large painting hanging on an interior wall. It was of an old clipper ship buffeted in storm-tossed seas, a collection of opaque grays, greens, ivory and brown.

"Does the painting interest you that much?"

The voice that came from directly behind her was husky and cynically amused. Amanda turned, unconscious of the hands clenched tightly in front of her. His gaze was dark and brooding as it traveled the length of her body and stopped at her face.

"Are you nervous?" The harsh planes of his face, browned by the sun and made darker by the coal black of his hair and eyes, increased the primitive attraction that drew her to him.

"A little," she admitted, spreading her fingers and rubbing them together in an effort to relax.

Jarod Colby watched the movement with indifference, subtly making her aware of the breadth of his shoulders and his intimidating height. The throbbing of her pulse echoed loudly in her ears as coursing heat spread through her body. The soft music in the background added to the disturbing air of intimacy. The silence between them was threatening to suffocate her.

"Will you be leaving very early in the morning?" Amanda asked, trying to make her voice sound natural and not betray the tension that held her by the throat.

His eyes flicked back to her face. "Early enough."

"It must be hectic to commute back and forth."

"Yes."

His clipped reply sent her wildly searching for something else to say. How could she pursue a conversation that he wasn't willing to take part in? She broke away from his compelling gaze. Perhaps he didn't wish to discuss business.

"You have a beautiful home," Amanda murmured.

The comment passed unnoticed by him as he held out his hand to her. For a minute she blinked at it uncertainly, then hesitantly placed her own hand in it. The large hand closed warmly around her fingers, pulling her to him as an arm moved around her waist. He carried her fingers to his lips while he guided her to the slow tempo of the music. The brooding expression in his eyes didn't change as it moved possessively over her face.

Last night when they had danced, her hooped

skirt had kept considerable distance between them. Now Amanda was held tightly against him, her legs burning with the brush of his thighs while the softness of her breasts felt the imprint of the buttons of his shirt. She hadn't been prepared for the contact of his body, hard and muscular and very male. Her head was tilted back, exposing the bareness of her throat as she watched his lips move over her hand in a caress that had her whole arm tingling.

There was an unreal quality about the moment, a dreamlike magic that sent her senses spinning. The hand resting near his shoulders could feel the taut muscles in the arm that circled her waist. The nibbling of her fingers ceased as he turned her hand to expose her sensitive palm and pressed a warm kiss in its hollow. The sensual touch of his tongue against her skin released an avalanche of churning emotions inside her. Exhaling slowly in surrender, Amanda dipped her head against his chest, all resistance flowing out of her weakened limbs.

Leaving her hand against the shaven smoothness of his face, Jarod trailed his fingers firmly down her arm and up to her shoulder, caressing her flesh with controlled firmness. Of its own volition, her hand remained on his face, her fingertips exploring the jutting line of his jaw and the sharp cheekbones. There was no urgency in the languid passion between them, even though the slow-burning flame kept growing hotter as his mouth trailed down her face to the lobe of her ear.

After interminable minutes his mouth sought

hers, not in a gentle probing caress but in a demanding, hungry kiss. Her hands were locked around his neck as she stood on tiptoe, instinctively arching her back to be closer to the lean hardness of his body. In sweet ecstasy, Amanda knew she had been kissed with passion before, but she couldn't recall returning more than a small part of it until now. A warning bell rang in her head, pulling her out of the whirling ache of desire.

"Jarod, please!" Her lips moved in protest against his mouth. Her senses felt drugged by his kiss, unable to function without the union of their lips.

He let her move partially out of his arms, the smoldering fire in his eyes nearly sending her back into them. "What is it?" he demanded.

His voice was hoarse and his breathing was uneven, and Amanda could feel the iron control he had over his emotions. Oddly that hurt. She wanted him to be as destroyed by her touch as she was by his.

"The music's stopped," she murmured, suddenly at a loss to admit how deeply she had been affected by his embrace.

A scowl of annoyance flashed across his face, quickly replaced by an enigmatic look that Amanda couldn't fathom. His hands dropped to his side and he turned away, leaving her standing on wobbly legs that hadn't recovered completely from the devastating weakness of the previous moments.

"Go and change it, then." Jarod ordered smoothly.

She heard the snap of his lighter and saw the

smoke rise above his head. Forcing her trembling legs to support her, she walked to the stereo and flipped the record to the other side. When she turned around, she saw Jarod pouring liquid from a crystal decanter that had been sitting on one of the tables. His eyes met hers across the room.

"Would you like a drink?" he asked.

Amanda shook her head. "No thank you."

There was a brief arching of a dark brow as he took a hefty swallow of liquor, then refilled the partially empty glass and walked to a large chair, where he sat down. Amanda remained beside the stereo, unable to feel the nonchalance he was exhibiting. His eyes studied her with a penetrating thoroughness that sent a tidal wave of heat flooding over her.

"Come here," he ordered crisply.

Swallowing jerkily, she walked toward him, stopping beside his chair and gazing down at him. Her long hair fell forward across her face and she nervously tucked the red gold locks behind her ears. Jarod had evidently discarded his jacket while she had been changing the record because she was suddenly aware that only a white silk shirt covered his chest. Amanda watched as he impatiently removed his tie, tossing it on the table on the other side of him, and unbuttoned the top buttons of his shirt. The sight of the dark hairs curling on his chest sent her heart catapulting into her throat. She started to turn away, but his hand caught at her wrist.

"Your pulse is racing," he said.

"I know," Amanda murmured.

"Do I disturb you?"

With his eyes watching her so closely, she couldn't answer that question. To admit that he did would make her too vulnerable; to lie that he didn't was impossible.

His hand slid across the lower part of her stomach to rest on her hipbone. "You don't need to answer that question," Jarod said in a complacent voice. "I can feel the way your bones almost melt when I touch you."

Her startled eyes swept his face, but he was looking at the agitated movement of her breasts and the way the material covering them strained at the narrow straps supporting her dress.

"Jarod, please—" she began.

"Please what?" he growled. His eyes blazed upward to her face. "For twenty-four damn hours, I've been remembering the way those proper lips taunted me."

"Don't say that," she protested.

"Why not?" he snapped savagely, brutally yanking her off balance and pulling her across his lap. "Right now you feel as improper as I do. Why shouldn't we admit it?" A hand moved roughly over her hip to her back while she felt the thudding of his heart beneath her own hands. "I wanted to hold you like this last night. Do you deny that you didn't want it, too?"

"No," Amanda whispered.

"I couldn't forget the scent of your perfume or how soft your skin was when I touched it," he murmured, threading the fingers of one hand through her hair. "This morning it was even worse, being in a room with you, alone, and not taking you in my arms. Then earlier we had to waste so much time over that stupid meal. All the while I'm aching with the need to see and touch every inch of you.''

A whimpering moan slipped out of Amanda's lips at the blatant passion in his voice. His fingers automatically moved to the corner of her mouth and parted her lips while searing desire scorched her with the hottest blue flames.

His arms crushed her against him as he possessively demanded her complete response. The masterful caress of his hands over her thighs and hips, across her back and shoulders, aroused her to a fever pitch of longing. She felt like an addict who couldn't get enough of his kisses even as he ravaged and explored her mouth and neck, sending torrents of liquid fire through her veins.

A sudden release of all inhibitions seemed to enclose her in a velvet mist. Her head was tilted back over his arm while Jarod ran his mouth over her collarbone, pushing aside the offending strap and sliding it down her arm until it was permanently out of the way. Through the reeling of her mind, Amanda felt the brush of his fingertips in the hollow between her breasts. Instinctively she stiffened when the material of her dress slipped unresistingly down.

Instantly alert, no longer possessed by her drowning senses, she felt his hand sliding along her back, down the nakedness of her spine. With sickening swiftness she realized that the sensation of release she had experienced moments before had been the expert movements of Jarod's hand when he had unzipped her dress.

The suddenness of her lunge away from him was unexpected. She stumbled shakily to her feet, clutching the bodice tightly to her, her eyes shimmering with unshed tears of shame and uncertainty. Desire still blazed in the eyes he turned toward her, but it was quickly replaced by a confused anger as she backed away from him. She trembled with self-contempt over how close she had come to allowing him to seduce her. He must think she was some local tramp! She had behaved like one, responding wantonly to his advances.

CHAPTER FIVE

"I WANT TO GO HOME." Her voice was jerky with barely controlled sobs of humiliation.

Jarod rose to his feet, a black scowl clouding his face while he towered threateningly in front of her. Amanda would have fled then if she had believed her legs would support her.

"Why the display of outrage?" he demanded savagely, his lip curling at the tears that hovered on the edge of her lashes. "I made it clear I wanted you."

Had he? Yes, she supposed, he had, only she had been too inexperienced and blinded by the overwhelming attraction he held for her to understand the completeness of his statement. His anger was justified to that extent and she found she couldn't meet his eyes.

"I'm sorry," she murmured, looking anywhere in the room except at him. "I'm just not that kind of girl."

Contemptuous laughter rang harshly through the room. "Are you going to tell me you're a virgin?" he jeered sarcastically. "I don't believe that I'm the first man to touch you that way."

"It doesn't matter whether you believe me or not." Her throat was working convulsively.

Jarod moved with such striking swiftness that she wasn't able to avoid him as his hands reached out to dig into her shoulders and pull her viciously against him.

"You're lying!" his husky voice growled. "I don't give a damn! I don't have to be the first man. There's no need to play the innocent."

"I am not playing!" Amanda cried out bitterly. The painful sobs now came freely from her throat. "It's the truth! Now let me go!"

He shook her until her head was bobbing from side to side uncontrollably. "Is it money you want? Are you afraid I won't pay you?"

The violent shaking stopped and Amanda sagged limply in his hands. "What do you want for proof?" she sobbed weakly. "Shall I let you rape me?"

He grabbed a handful of her hair and pulled her head back to stare into her face. A muscle twitched near the corner of his eye where a glimmer of doubt lurked.

"Are you telling me the truth?" His voice was ominously quiet.

"Yes," she whispered.

There was a string of angry expletives as he abruptly released her and turned away. A hand savagely raked his hair. "From now on," Jarod muttered beneath his breath, his back still turned to her, "you'd better stick to the shallow water until you learn to swim."

Amanda was too embarrassed to reply as she struggled to slip the strap over her shoulder and make her shaking fingers rezip her dress. But her movements were awkward and uncoordinated, achieving little success. In the next minute, Jarod was turning her around and pushing her hands away.

"I've had more practice at this than you have," he jeered, closing the zipper with one fluid movement.

His fingers closed over her waist, firmly pivoting her around to face him. For one crazy moment she thought he was going to take her in his arms. As she brushed the tears from her cheeks, she realized that she wanted him to hold her and ease the ache in her heart.

"We'll forget about next Saturday night," he said tautly. "The less I see of you, the better."

"Of course," Amanda murmured as someone twisted the knife in her stomach.

"Come on, I'll take you home." Jarod was striding away from her toward the door and she followed meekly, scraping together what little dignity and self-respect that remained.

Jarod said not a word as he held the car door open for her, nor even when he slid behind the wheel a few minutes later. The sky was black with lingering clouds blocking out most of the stars and allowing the moon to peep out occasionally. As soon as Jarod reached the main road, he accelerated the car until the telephone poles were only a blur. Amanda knew he could hardly wait to get her home. When he finally pulled up at her home, the house was ablaze with lights.

"What time is it?" she asked nervously.

"Nearly ten." He hadn't switched the engine off.

Her family would be up, no doubt waiting to hear about her evening. Amanda began patting and smoothing her rumpled hair and trying to wipe away all traces of tears from her face. With an angry ejaculation, Jarod turned the ignition switch, shutting off the engine, and flipped down the visor in front of her, revealing a mirror on the other side.

"You're a mess," he muttered grimly. Rummaging through the glove compartment, he paused to hand her a comb.

The reflection in the mirror confirmed his statement. Even in the dim nightglow, Amanda could see the smudged streaks on her face where the mascara had run. Her hair was so rumpled and tousled it looked as if she had just climbed out of bed. As she remedied that with the comb, she saw Jarod tearing open a tiny packet that contained one of those commercially packaged wet towels.

"Turn around." His fingers gripped her chin to ensure that she did as he commanded.

"Why are you doing this?" Amanda whispered. The stringent scent of soap-filled wetness acted as reviving smelling salts as he roughly wiped the traces of mascara from her cheeks. "Why do you care what my family will think?"

His eyes gleamed cynically at her through the darkness. "Because I don't want to be forced to find a new manager at the mill."

"You know who my father is?" she breathed.

"There are several families named Bennett in Oak Springs."

"But only one with a red-haired daughter." Jarod looked at her derisively. "Did you think I hadn't checked on you? The names of your two nieces are Teresa and Jennifer. Would you like their birth dates, or your grade point average in college?"

Hysterical laughter bubbled inside her. "I should be honored that you found me fit company. What a pity you picked me for your night's entertainment!"

"Who would guess that a woman could reach the age of twenty-one in these liberated times and remain innocent? You should enter a convent," he sneered.

His taunt demanded retaliation, and Amanda struck out with her hand at the features of chiseled bronze. Needle-sharp barbs stung her palm as it made contact with his cheek. Her heart leaped in fear at the gathering mask of black fury. She pushed open the door and scrambled out of the car, but Jarod was sliding out her side and caught her before she was a step away. He pulled her against the tapering length of his body. Wild tremors shivered through her as she struggled to elude the mouth descending toward hers, but it closed over her lips and punishingly devoured them.

There was a sudden blaze of light from the porch followed by the laughing voices of her parents, then shocked silence. At the first sound, Jarod had thrust her away from him, but not before her parents, sister, and grandfather had seen the way they had been molded together. Pain from the cruel grip of Jarod's fingers digging into her waist kept Amanda from dashing into the house.

"Good evening, Mr. Bennett," Jarod greeted him calmly.

"Mr. Colby," her father returned with a nod, recovering as quickly as Jarod had. "I must apologize for our intrusion. None of us heard your car drive up, and Amanda hasn't been home from a date at this hour since she was sixteen."

"I have an early flight in the morning," Jarod replied, as if that was the explanation. "It was nice meeting you, Mrs. Bennett." His head moved briefly in the direction of her mother before he turned it to Amanda. Only she was close enough to see the freezing coldness in his eyes. "Amanda," he murmured with patronizing politeness.

"Good night." She forced the words from her throat.

She used the precious moments that it took for him to get in his car and drive away to gather her wits before walking to the porch where her family waited. Her grandfather was grumbling about Yankees under his breath while shuffling toward a rocking chair as Amanda slowly climbed the porch steps. No one spoke.

"I've had a hectic day. I...I think I'll go ahead and turn in," she murmured, knowing she was fooling none of them, but her parents let her go with curious looks and nods of good night.

All except her younger sister Bonnie, who trailed

after her as Amanda walked into the house. "Where did you go? What did you do?" Bonnie whispered excitedly. "If he'd held me like that, I'd be absolutely devastated! When will he be back? Do you suppose he'll call you while he's gone?"

Amanda pressed her fingers against her forehead, feeling that any moment she would snap in two. "Bonnie, please," she protested with a tortured cry, "I have an awful headache. I don't feel like talking tonight."

A look of stunned pain crossed her sister's face. After either one of them had come home from a date, they had always got together for an hour of girl talk. Now Amanda was shutting her out.

"I'm sorry," Amanda murmured, and raced up the stairs to her room.

With the door securely closed behind her, she wished her memory had a self-destructive button so she could wipe away the events of the evening and forget what a complete fool she had made of herself. Her arms wound themselves tightly around her as she tried to forget the thrill she had experienced under Jarod's expert caress. But she had only to close her eyes to feel the sensual pressure of his lips on her and the answering surge of warmth from her middle.

There was a light rap on her door in warning before her mother walked into the room, enabling Amanda to start unzipping her dress as though she had been in the act of changing her clothes.

"Hello, mom," she said, striving for indifference.

"Bonnie said you had a headache. Is there anything wrong?"

"It's only tension," Amanda answered with a shrug, reaching into the closet for a hanger to put her dress on.

"I hope we didn't embarrass you tonight. We honestly didn't know you were out there."

"I know."

"Your Mr. Colby seems like a very nice man."

"He's not my Mr. Colby!" Amanda snapped, and immediately covered her mouth as she turned her rounded brown eyes on her mother. "Sorry—I didn't mean to shout at you."

A tiny frown made worried lines on her mother's face. "Will you be seeing him again, Mandy?"

It all became too much for her. Amanda couldn't keep up the pretense that nothing was wrong. Her shoulders hunched forward as she cradled her churning stomach in her arms.

"No, mother." Her head moved painfully from side to side. "I won't be seeing him again."

She felt the touch of her mother's hands on her shoulders and turned instinctively for the comfort they promised. She suddenly didn't feel like an adult.

"Do you want to, Mandy?" her mother asked softly, cradling the silent girl against her breast, feeling the pain that was transmitted.

"Yes." Then, "No, I don't." Amanda straightened and breathed in deeply. She wasn't going to let herself cry. Not again.

"Tonight—" Mrs. Bennett began hesitantly,

picking up the vibrations of conflicting emotions warring inside her daughter.

"Tonight was a mistake that neither Jarod nor I want to repeat," Amanda sighed. "I really am tired, mom."

"All right, dear. No more questions." The older woman smiled and brushed her cheek with a fleeting kiss before leaving the room.

"WHICH ONE OF YOU GIRLS is going to pick up your father?" Mrs. Bennett called from the back door of the house.

Amanda glanced at Bonnie. "Don't look at me," her sister said. "As soon as I finish watering the garden, I'm going in the house to water myself. You go and get dad."

"Okay," Amanda agreed, rubbing the sore muscles of her lower back. "Hose my legs off, but for heaven's sake don't get my shorts wet because I don't want to change my clothes."

Bonnie obligingly turned the nozzle toward her sister, letting the water spray over the lower part of Amanda's legs while avoiding the red material of her shorts. Water squished in Amanda's canvas shoes, but it felt refreshingly cool after two hours in the hot afternoon sun.

"The last of the beans are inside the back door, mom," Amanda called. "Where are the car keys?"

"They're still in the car," her mother answered.

"Be back soon!"

Waving to Bonnie, Amanda backed the car out of the driveway and headed it for the mill. The man her father usually rode back and forth to work with was home with the flu. Rather than leave the rest of his family without transportation, her father decided to have one of them drive him to work in the morning and pick him up at night.

After Amanda had parked the car in front of the cotton mill, she glanced in the rearview mirror to be sure there weren't any smudges of dirt on her face from working in the garden. Spending five days a week in long dress, it was nice on Monday and Tuesday, the days Oak Run was closed to tourists, to run around in shorts and knit tops, especially in this hot June weather. She slipped the car keys into the small pocket of her shorts and walked gaily to the door marked Private. One hand rapped lightly while the other turned the knob and opened the door.

"Hi, dad. Are you ready to go?"

Three steps inside the office, Amanda came to an abrupt halt as she stared at Jarod Colby standing beside her father's desk. She knew her face had grown pale, although there was practically no reaction on his. Her father was sitting in his chair, his gaze taking in the stunned look of surprise on her face.

"Have a chair. I'll only be a couple of minutes," he told her.

After one brief glance at her when she had walked in the door, Jarod had turned his attention to the paper spread in front of him on the desk. Since he had chosen not to greet her, Amanda ignored him, as well. Her legs numbly welcomed the support of the chair behind her.

For three weeks she had attempted to block out every humiliating memory of what had happened. It had just begun to take on the vague horror of a bad dream, and here she was in the same room with him, feeling her bones turning to water at the sight of his raven dark hair and eyes and the virile, masculine face. The cream tan suit he was wearing accentuated the leanness of his physique and she knew she would never be able to forget what that muscular hardness had felt like pressed against her own body.

The two men were discussing the contents of the papers Jarod was studying, but Amanda was in too much of a daze to hear what they were saying. Someone knocked at the office door and she nearly jumped out of her chair.

"Can I see you a minute, Mr. Bennett?" a man requested, opening the door but not entering the room.

"Is it important, Joe?" her father asked.

"Yes, sir."

Her father darted a look to Amanda, then brought his gaze back to Jarod, who was concentrating on one of the papers. "Excuse me a minute, Mr. Colby."

"I'm in no hurry, Sam," Jarod replied, glancing briefly from the papers on the desk.

When the door closed behind her father, the room became uncomfortably still. Amanda sat hesitantly on the edge of her chair, afraid to breathe and draw those dark eyes her way. Then Jarod thrust his hands in his pockets and walked around to the front of the desk, where he leaned against it and let his eyes wander calmly over her bare legs to her face.

"Hello, Amanda," he said.

"Mr. Colby," she murmured, dipping her head self-consciously in greeting.

"The last time we met, I think we went beyond the point of 'Mister.'" One side of his mouth lifted in a mirthless, almost derisive smile.

"Please, I'm...I'm not proud of the way I acted that night," Amanda protested. Her cheeks felt hot and flushed and she bent her head to conceal them from his penetrating gaze. "After the way I behaved, it was natural for you to get the wrong impression. If you'll excuse me," she said, rising agitatedly to her feet, "I'll wait for my father in the car."

"No, wait," he commanded.

"Look," she began nervously, "I didn't know you were going to be here. If I had, I wouldn't have come in."

"I know," Jarod replied with the same blandness as before. "I came in as your father was phoning home to have someone come to get him. I had a feeling it would be you, so I waited."

Her brown eyes rounded with surprise. "You waited? Why?"

"I discovered that I wanted to see you again." His gaze was making another cool appraisal of her.

For a moment Amanda couldn't breathe. The blood raced in her temples, sounding like a thousand snare drums in her ears. She could sense he was gauging her reaction to his statement. She had humiliated herself once and she wasn't going to do it again.

Drawing herself up to her full height, which still left her several inches shorter than him, she replied, "You were correct the last time when you said the less we saw of each other, the better."

He leisurely crossed the small space between them. "When you deprive yourself of chocolate, you always remember the sweet taste. But if you stuff yourself with it until it makes you sick—" there was a hard, mocking glint in his eyes "—then you lose your craving."

"I'm not a piece of chocolate!" she declared, taking a step backward as he took another forward.

Jarod kept advancing and Amanda kept retreating until she felt the metal of a filing cabinet behind her.

"The principle is the same. I want to see you again."

When she started to move sideways, he placed an arm on each side of her, blocking the path of escape.

"I don't want to see you," she stated firmly, pressing herself against the metal cabinet, her fingers clutching the smooth sides in desperation.

"You've felt the force of the attraction we hold for each other," Jarod murmured. "You can't bury your head in the sand and pretend it doesn't exist."

That languorous weakness was flowing through her again, but she grimly clung to her self-respect, fighting off the rush of desire his nearness was causing. As if he guessed the power he held over her senses, he moved closer, the pressure of his thighs against her adding fuel to the raging fire in her veins. The male smell of him was an erotic stimulant, arousing her and reminding her that she could never be indifferent. She closed her eyes against the arrogant dark head moving inexorably toward hers.

His mouth traveled lightly down the side of her face to her lips. "Friday night we'll drive to Atlanta, take in a show." The movement of his lips as he spoke sensually teased the sensitive corner of her mouth.

"No," she whispered weakly, twisting her head away, only to have him pursue.

"There's a dance at the club on Saturday," he murmured. The width of an angel's hair was all that separated her from the promising ardor of his kiss. She lacked the strength to turn away again as his mouth continued the tantalizing movement against the trembling weakness of hers. "On Saturday we'll drive to the coast and spend the day."

It was becoming increasingly impossible not to make that one tiny movement that would give him possession of her lips. "I have to work on Sunday," Amanda declared breathlessly, fighting through the blackness swirling around her to cling to her sanity.

Soft laughter fanned her face. "I own Oak Run," Jarod reminded her. "I can close it for the day. We'll swim in the Atlantic and sunbathe on the beach—with clothes, if your modesty demands it."

A sighing moan quaked through her at the same moment that footsteps sounded outside the office door, followed imediately by the rattle of the knob. Prior to the door's opening, Jarod levered himself away, letting one arm fall to his side as he half turned toward her father. The gold tips of her lashes fluttered upward, disturbed brown eyes immediately focusing on the implacable profile of the man leaning beside her. A darting glance at her father caught the quizzical expression in his gaze. Her cheeks colored in a rare blush.

"I'll...I'll wait for you in the car, dad," Amanda stammered, eluding the darkness of Jarod's gaze as she hurried for the door.

When she reached the car, her breath was coming in jerky gulps. Another minute—another second and she would have given in. She bit hard into her trembling lips, still afire from the tantalizing feather caress of his. He was playing at a game of which he was master. It was of little consequence that she affected him physically, too, because she didn't possess the power to annihilate his control, while he completely swamped hers.

Her breathing had regained a degree of normalcy when the two men walked out of the office. Without a glance in her direction, Jarod walked by the car to his own. Involuntarily her eyes watched as he drove away before she became aware of her father sitting behind the wheel of the car, his hand outstretched for the ignition keys.

"You look tired, dad," she murmured with a false smile as she handed him the keys from her pocket. "Did you have a rough day?"

The corners of his mouth lifted in wry amusement. "I didn't think you'd noticed me at all, but yes, it was a long day."

Amanda shifted uncomfortably, her eyes straying toward the dust cloud left by Jarod's car. "That's not true," she protested, but without conviction.

"Isn't it? I had the distinct impression that I was creating an unwanted crowd of three."

"Did Jarod—I mean, Mr. Colby say that?"

"The only comment Mr. Colby made—" his voice gave extra inflection to the "Mister" "—was that I had a strong willed and beautiful daughter."

That statement did nothing to untangle the knots her stomach was in. Her gaze shifted self-consciously to the slowly passing scenery outside the window of the now moving car.

"What do you think of him, daddy?" she asked quietly.

There was a pause before her father answered, then it was with deliberation. "You're an adult, Amanda. What do you think of him?"

"That he's out of my class," she sighed heavily.

"Inverted snobbery?"

He had misinterpreted her reply and she was just as glad. It would be difficult to explain the physical impact Jarod made on her. It was something she wasn't used to herself.

"I suppose you could call it that," she agreed. "You have to admit the world of Colby Enterprises is far removed from ours."

"No so far that we're not a part of it," he

reminded her. "If you want to see the man again, don't let feelings of inadequacy stop you."

That was easily said, she thought. Inadequacy walked hand in hand with inexperience in this case. There was frightened triumph in knowing he wanted to see her again, but Amanda wasn't convinced that she could emerge unscathed from another encounter with Jarod Colby. Rather than be trapped by an emotional upheaval she couldn't control, she decided it was best not to go out with him again, no matter how much she was drawn to him.

CHAPTER SIX

HER DECISION WAS TESTED later that evening when the telephone rang and Bonnie announced that it was for her. Before she reached the receiver, Amanda guessed it would be Jarod.

"Is seven o'clock too early for Friday night?" his voice asked the minute she had identified herself.

"I'm not going with you," she answered in a low voice.

"Saturday?"

"No."

"Don't play hard to get, Amanda." The telephone lines didn't soften the harshness in his tone.

"I'm not." She had to make her replies short and clipped in order to conceal her shaking voice. "The answer is no. Tomorrow. Next week. Next month. No!"

She heard the savage intake of breath. "I don't accept that. And you don't want me to," he snapped. "You proved that today."

There was no answer to that statement. He was too accustomed to overcoming a woman's objection not to know he had been on the brink of succeeding that afternoon. Very slowly Amanda replaced the receiver on the hook, afraid that if she talked to him any longer, he would somehow still succeed.

"That was Jarod Colby, wasn't it?" The sound of her sister's voice brought Amanda round. "And you just turned him down? You're either insane or ingenious!"

Amanda's lips tightened fractionally. "I don't want to get on board a fast train going nowhere, Bonnie," she replied. "If he calls back, tell him I'm not here."

But Jarod didn't call back. With each day that passed, Amanda became more convinced that he had taken her answer as final. Yet her second meeting with him had effectively diminished the humiliating recriminations of the first. By turning him down, she had thought to bolster her pride and her sense of integrity. Instead she found herself wishing she hadn't been so adamant in her refusal. He had wanted to see her again, and if she was honest with herself, she wanted to see him.

It wasn't so important anymore that any relationship with him would be doomed to failure at the start. If marriage figured anywhere in his plans for the future, it wouldn't be to a small-town girl like her. Nor would he be satisfied with an innocent and—compared to the relationships he undoubtedly had with other women—what would amount to a platonic association with her. Amanda had considered herself a liberated woman, intent on a career that she planned to continue after she was married, and open-minded toward her friends' more intimate relationships with their boyfriends. Her own chaste state she had marked off to the fact that she had never met a man she cared for deeply enough, and experimenting for the sake of experience wasn't one of her traits.

Faced with the alternative of having an affair with Jarod Colby should she see him again, which looked unlikely with each passing day, Amanda wondered how deeply she cared for him. Was she still wrapped up in her illusions of the past? Was the attraction purely physical between them? Or was there a chance of deeper emotions being involved? If there was, she had the depressing feeling that it would only be on her side.

Such gloomy thoughts, she chided herself idly. But they matched the day, gray and dreary with a slow drizzle coming out of the overcast sky, the misty rain alleviating none of the sticky humidity. Few tourists would be tramping around this afternoon in such dismal weather.

"Pam." Amanda turned from the window to the trio of girls chattering in the corner. "Why don't you and Susan go on home? Linda and I will stay until closing. I don't expect a sudden deluge of visitors to appear."

"Great!" Pam replied as she and Susan rose eagerly to their feet. "I have to wash my hair. Heaven only knows if it'll dry in this weather."

"A car is pulling up out front," Linda announced with a sigh. "Wouldn't you know there'd be some fools wandering around in this gluck!"

Amanda sighed, too, but in relief. She didn't like having so much time on her hands to think. Everyone in town knew she had gone out with Jarod Colby, including her three co-workers. Each time she had tried to join in the light conversations about clothes or music or men, they shifted the subject to Jarod, exhibiting curiosity, envy and a touch of malice that Amanda hadn't been out with him again. Not even for the sake of her pride would she confide that she had turned him down. It was something they wouldn't understand or believe.

"How many people are there?" Amanda asked, nodding to the departing girls moving down the hall as she sifted through the brochures that were given to each visitor.

"Two. A man and a woman," Linda answered, peering through the sheer folds of the curtain. Then she gasped loudly. "Amanda!" she squeaked excitedly. "I think it's Jarod Colby!"

Unconsciously Amanda stiffened, half noticing that the other two girls had stopped to turn around, their eyes staring at her to see her reaction. Blood rushed quickly into her face and just as quickly receded as the front door opened.

Jarod was not the first one to walk in. A stunning brunette preceded him wearing a pantsuit Amanda knew she could never afford if she saved a whole year. It didn't help to notice the material was a perfect match for the sapphire blue eyes. The woman was more than beautiful, with the sophistication of a model, and it was evident that she was very well acquainted with Jarod.

"Good afternoon, Miss Bennett." His jeering voice swung her eyes around to him, pain in their brown depths as she met the hard indifference of his gaze. He was casually dressed in close-fitting black trousers and a silk shirt in swirling shades of gray.

"Good afternoon, Mr. Colby. What a surprise to see you here." Even to her own ears, her voice sounded brittle and false. Amanda didn't need to glance around to feel the unconcealed interest of the other girls in the exchange between her and Jarod.

His gaze turned to the brunette securely attached to his arm. "Vanessa has never been through Oak Run. I thought this would be a perfect day for her to take a leisurely tour of the plantation house, considering the shortage of visitors you seem to have."

"The weather is keeping them away," Amanda murmured defensively. "You and—" she stopped and regathered her wits "—the two of you will have the place to yourselves. I hope you enjoy your tour." The last comment was directed to the brunette, who was regarding her with ill-concealed amusement.

There was a sardonic glint in Jarod's eyes as he brought them to bear on Amanda. "I believe you've misunderstood me, Miss Bennett," he said dryly. "I'll be using your office to make a few phone calls. Rather than have Miss Scott become bored waiting for me—"

"As if I could, darling!" the woman murmured, smiling provocatively into his face.

"—I thought to keep her amused with a tour of Oak Run," Jarod finished after returning the inviting smile.

"Of course," Amanda agreed tightly. Her fin-

gernails were making marks in her palms. Every
nerve end in her body screamed with jealousy.
There was a primitive urge to scratch at those
sparkling blue eyes gazing so rapturously at Jarod.
Stiffly Amanda turned to Linda, her mouth forming the words to order her to conduct the brunette
through the house. "Linda, would you—"

Jarod's voice broke in. "As you're the senior
guide, I would prefer that you show Vanessa
around, Miss Bennett."

Her head jerked back to him, indignant anger
blazing in her eyes. "Is that an order, Mr. Colby?" she demanded.

She didn't need to hear the sudden intake of
breath from her fellow guides to know that her
tone of voice was not one that she should use to
address her employer. The aloofly cynical mask
had fallen from Jarod's face as his nostrils flared
in anger. Black fire flamed in his eyes.

"Yes, Miss Bennett, it is," he snapped.

Fighting off the desire to run from the house
rather than escort his mistress, or whatever she
was, through the building, Amanda moved to
comply with his edict. The long skirt of her ruffled
gown gave a regal grace to her carriage and added
to the proudly defiant tilt of her head.

"Will you come this way, Miss Scott?" she requested in a coolly polite tone, not waiting for the
girl's amused nod of assent as she started down the
hall.

The need to escape the lacerating sardonicism of
Jarod's gaze prompted Amanda to change the
usual procedure of the tour, which had always

begun with the first-floor rooms, by leading the woman to the staircase. In her best professional voice, she began her recitation.

"As we go up the stairs to the second floor, you will notice indentations and scars on the original oak steps. These disfiguring marks are believed to have been caused by Union soldiers riding their horses through the house when it was first taken."

The tour of the second floor took very little time, with Vanessa Scott exhibiting only desultory interest in the priceless furniture and the ornate canopy beds. The woman's attitude seemed to be one of indifference until Amanda led her back down the stairs.

"Which room is the ballroom?" the woman inquired, glancing idly around at the various doors that led off the main hall. "I'd like to see it."

Usually that was one of the last rooms shown before a tour was taken upstairs, but since Amanda had already rearranged the route once, she saw no point in not doing it again.

"It's through these doors," she said, walking ahead of the girl to open them. She opened her mouth to begin describing some of the antiques in the room when she was interrupted.

"Is this where the cotillion is held?"

"Yes," Amanda answered politely. "Since the early 1900s, there's been a dance, or cotillion as we call it, in celebration of Jefferson Davis's birthday."

"Have you ever been to one?" For the first time since the confrontation in the hall, Vanessa's blue eyes turned their speculative gleam away from her surroundings to study Amanda.

"Yes, I have. It's quite a festive occasion. A string quartet provides the music and all the guests are required to wear costumed dress of the Old South days." Amanda artfully used the personal question to describe the atmosphere of the ball, hoping to sidetrack further questions of a similar nature. "The style of dresses is very similar to the ones we tour guides wear, only much more elaborate."

"With your red hair, you must have worn green," the girl commented.

"Yes, I did. Now, if you will notice the chandeliers on each end of the room, they were imported—"

"Did you meet Jarod's cousin Judith?"

Amanda stopped her speech and turned slowly around to face the attractive brunette. Seething anger was nearing the boiling point.

"No, I did not," she answered, and waited for the next question.

"How well do you know Jarod?"

"I barely know him at all, Miss Scott," Amanda replied coldly and truthfully. "I'm employed by his corporation as a guide in his home."

"And that's all?" The blue gaze flicked arrogantly over her face, deliberately baiting and derisive. "I understand from Judith, who is a very dear personal friend of mine, that Jarod caused quite a sensation the night of the cotillion with the attention he paid to a certain redhead in an emerald green gown. Could that have been you?"

"As I recall, I did dance one dance with Mr. Colby." Ice dripped from Amanda's voice.

"It's hardly something you're likely to forget, is it?" Vanessa suggested dryly. "Did he ask you out?"

Amanda's jaw clamped down tightly, allowing her reply to slip out through gritted teeth. "That is personal and none of your business!"

"It seems to be the whole town's business. And everything that has to do with Jarod I make my business." A sickeningly sweet smile was directed at Amanda, who was already beginning to feel nauseated by the entire conversation. "You see, Jarod has his little flings from time to time."

"Since they never seem to last and he obviously keeps running back to you," Amanda murmured sarcastically, "what's the point or purpose of this discussion?"

"None, really." Slender shoulders were shrugged negligently. "I was merely curious to see who the little country charmer was."

"Now that you've accomplished that, there isn't any reason to continue the tour." Under normal circumstances Amanda would have never allowed her cold rage to lead to rudeness to any visitor to Oak Run, but the woman's tone of superiority drove her to striking back. "I think the charade has gone far enough. You are no more interested in seeing the house than I am to show it to you. I'm sure you would much rather get back to your darling Jarod." Her voice was beginning to shake with the violence of her anger. "I must say the two of you are very well suited to each other. You're both arrogant, conceited, egotistical—"

"That's enough, Miss Bennett!" a rough voice barked behind her.

Amanda spun around to stare at the murderous expression on Jarod's face. Her heart gave a wild, frightened leap at the unrelenting harshness in his eyes.

"Oh, darling—" Vanessa Scott moved swiftly forward to place a hand on his arm "—I'm sorry you had to hear such—"

"Would you wait for me in the car, please. I want to speak to Miss Bennett alone," he interrupted coldly.

"Of course," the girl murmured, flashing a triumphant look at Amanda before withdrawing from the room.

Amanda's brown eyes couldn't meet the contempt in his and she quickly lowered her gaze after Vanessa had left them alone. "I'll save you the trouble of firing me. I quit," she snapped.

"I don't give a damn whether you quit or not! I want an explanation for your rudeness to Miss Scott!"

"I lost my temper!" she shouted back.

"That's an excuse, not an explanation." He lowered his voice, but it still vibrated loudly in her ears. "I want to know why you treated a visitor with such insolence, Miss Bennett."

Amanda wearily pushed the hair away from her forehead, pain jabbing at her lungs. "Stop calling me that," she muttered in frustration, unwilling to admit that the discussion leading up to her attack

had been about him for fear he would think she
had started it.

"What do you suggest I call you?" he jeered
sarcastically. "Amanda?"

The contempt in his voice hurt more than she
cared to admit. "I suppose it really doesn't matter," she sighed.

"No, it doesn't," Jarod snapped. Silence
crushed them for an eternity of seconds. "I'm
waiting for your explanation."

"What do you want me to say?" she demanded
angrily. "How did you expect me to react when
you paraded your latest mistress in front of me?
What was I supposed to do? Smile and nod as if
she was just another stranger?"

"Why should it matter to you?" His dark head
was thrown back and he was looking arrogantly
down at her. "You made it very clear the last time
I talked to you that you wanted nothing more to
do with me. Didn't you mean it?"

"Yes, I meant it," Amanda confirmed nervously, regretting her jealous outburst of a second ago.

His hands closed around her waist while a compelling light glittered in his eyes. "Did you?"

"Yes," she answered in a very tiny voice.

"I don't think you did." A thick black brow
arched complacently. "I believe you would like to
go out with me again."

Amanda gazed helplessly into his face, so bluntly chiseled, so ruggedly masculine. The magic of
his touch was beginning to work its spell on her.

"I won't beg you," Jarod went on. "I'll ask you
one last time. The answer is either yes or no."

It was an ultimatum. Amanda knew he would never ask again. It was a second chance if she wanted it. She did—and yet. . . .

I would like to, but—'' she began nervously.

"Then you name the day, the place, and the time.''

"Monday.'' She breathed in deeply, braving the darkness of his gaze. "At one o'clock. We can spend the afternoon at Stone Mountain.''

A sound of disgust rolled from Jarod's throat as he removed his hands from her waist and started to turn away. She caught at one of his hands and held it between her own, unconsciously caressing the curling hairs on the back of it.

"Jarod, I—'' Amanda swallowed to ease the constriction in her throat "—I want to see you somewhere public.''

His gaze watched the movement of her hands before it flicked aloofly to her upturned face. "Where I can't take advantage of you, is that it?'' he asked.

"Yes, something like that,'' she admitted. His mockery made her feel so uncomfortably adolescent.

"I'll pick you up Monday at one.'' He slipped his hand from her unresisting hold and walked to the door.

"Jarod?'' Her questioning call halted him at the threshold to the hall. He half turned to look back at her, his expression unrevealingly cool. "Do I still have a job?'' she asked nervously.

"Frankly, I don't care.''

Her head jerked back at the sting of his tone.

Amanda pivoted quickly around so he couldn't see the effect his cruel indifference had on her.

"Damn!" he muttered under his breath, striding angrily to spin her around. His glowering look did little to assuage the tears burning the back of her eyes. "I don't interfere in the running of Oak Run. This is my aunt's pet project and she does the hiring and firing. If you want to hand in your resignation, give it to her."

"I have to work to help with my college expenses this fall," Amanda told him weakly.

The line of his eyes and mouth narrowed in exasperation. "I can't make up my mind if you're a schoolgirl or a woman!" he growled. "Keep your job, if that's what you want!"

Color flamed hotly beneath her skin. "Your work and your money are important to you. Why does it make me a schoolgirl if I feel the same?" she demanded. "Or are you simply regretting that you agreed to go out with a backcountry charmer like me?"

"Who called you that?" Amanda's mouth clamped tightly shut at his sharp inquiry. "Vanessa did, didn't she? That's why you retaliated with that outburst I overheard. So I finally got my explanation. I'll see you on Monday."

This time Jarod didn't stop at the hall door, but continued out of the mansion. Amanda was slower in leaving the ballroom, appearing in the hall after his car had left.

"Are you fired?" Linda asked in wide-eyed wonder. "I couldn't help overhearing part of what was said."

"No, I'm not," Amanda sighed in answer.

By the end of the week, she knew, the story of what happened today would be all over town. It would be useless to ask Linda to say nothing. There was more than one price to pay for seeing Jarod Colby, she realized. The fact that she was the first local girl he had shown any interest in only made the gossips more avidly malicious.

CHAPTER SEVEN

RISING ABOVE THE Georgia pines was a dome-shaped monolith, resembling the petrified remains of a great gray whale, five hundred and eighty-three acres of solid granite. Into its side was carved the sculpture of three of the most famous men in the short-lived history of the Confederate States of America: Jefferson Davis, president of the Confederacy; Stonewall Jackson, a general in the rebel army; and Robert E. Lee, a general and commander of all the Confederate armies. The entire work, the size of a city block, with the figure of Lee nearly as tall as a nine-story building, appeared the size of a postage stamp when compared to the immense proportions of Stone Mountain itself.

Amanda leaned back against Jarod's arm, his hand resting near the waistband of her lemon yellow slacks. As many times as she had seen the sculpture, she was still awed by its impressive size.

"Isn't it ironic," she said, glancing into his face, "that Gutzon Borglum, who was first commissioned to do this carving in the 1920s, left in frustration after roughing in the figure of Lee and later became so famous for his work at Mount Rushmore in the Black hills of South Dakota.

Here he was supposed to do the men of the Confederacy and there he completed the faces of four famous presidents of the United States, including Abraham Lincoln.''

"Have you seen Mount Rushmore?" Jarod asked.

"No," she answered with a shake of her head as a woman bumped into her and quickly apologized.

"It's getting a bit crowded here. Let's go somewhere else," he suggested, his arm propelling her away from the viewing patio below the sculpture. "Where to now? Do you want to visit the game farm where you can feed the animals? Go on a train ride or tour the plantation?"

The dryness of his voice revealed the subtle sarcasm hidden in his tone. Crowds of tourists everywhere and Amanda marveled at her own audacity in asking him to bring her here.

"We could go over to the carillon, I suppose," she said, shrugging.

"Do you think it's safer to walk or drive?"

"I'd rather walk." They skirted Memorial Hall, sometimes following the wake of other departing tourists and other times going against the flow of those arriving. "I'm sorry, Jarod. It wasn't a very good idea to come here, was it?"

"Considering you wanted to use the crowds to insulate yourself from me, I think it was an excellent idea," he contradicted her mockingly. "I'm surprised you're willing to allow me to hold your hand."

"Stop making me feel more miserable than I already am." Her gaze unhappily studied the pavement.

"This was your idea," Jarod reminded her. "What were we supposed to accomplish today?"

"I wanted to get to know you better, to find out more about you than just the fact that you own Colby Enterprises." Her voice was uneven.

"I can think of better places than this," he muttered bitterly.

"Let's forget the carillon and take me home. This whole thing is a disaster."

"Hardly a disaster," he murmured, although he shifted their direction to take them to the parking lot and his car. "You did learn something about me today."

"That you don't like crowds." A grimace pulled down the corners of her mouth.

"That, and the fact that I'm willing to put up with them in order to persuade you to meet me halfway." A light flickered briefly in his eyes before he turned his gaze away from her. "As beautiful as this park is, I can't say that I'm sorry to leave."

"Is that why you came today?" Disbelief was in her upturned face.

"I know you're frightened of me. It's there sometimes in those brown eyes of yours." Jarod opened the car door and helped her in while she digested his statement. The truth was she was afraid of herself.

"We don't have very much in common," she asserted as he slid behind the wheel and started the car.

"I have to breathe, eat and sleep the same as you. The only difference is I may have steak more often than you do." His mouth curved in amusement. "Having money doesn't set a man apart or make him better than others who don't have as much." Her face was a study of amazement when he glanced her way. "You look surprised."

"I never expected to hear Jarod Colby say such a thing."

"You did call me arrogant and conceited the other day. I am accustomed to getting what I want," Jarod admitted wryly, "mostly because I won't take no for an answer."

"Once you get something, do you still want it?"

"What are you asking?" Dark eyes moved over her face. "Do you want to know how long I'll keep you around after I know you better? That's a question I don't have the answer for yet."

"At least you're honest about it." Amanda breathed out slowly.

"I try to be honest about everything. I told you in the beginning that I wanted you. I wouldn't be here today if it weren't still true." His comment was made almost indifferently and Amanda found herself coloring at his candor. "How do you feel about me?"

"I don't know if I like you." She spoke hesitantly, staring straight ahead as he drove easily through the heavy traffic. "I'm attracted to you physically, but I can't make up my mind about you."

"Don't take too long." Beneath the teasing note

in his voice she sensed a hidden threat, an ominous assertion that he wouldn't wait forever for her decision.

The traffic was heavy during the journey back to Oak Springs. There seemed little necessity for conversation until Jarod stopped the car in front of Amanda's house. Shifting his weight, he stretched his arm along the back of the seat and looked at her.

"Now that we've dispensed with some of your nervousness, will you have dinner with me tomorrow night? At a public restaurant, if that will ease your mind further," he added with a wicked gleam dancing in his eyes.

"I'd like to, yes," Amanda agreed. The movement of her mouth brought dimples into play. "Thank you for today."

"Don't let my patience go unrewarded." His fingers closed over her shoulder and slowly drew her toward him. He took her lips in a lingering kiss, then gently pushed her back to her own side of the car.

Her hand closed over the door handle of the car. "What time will you be here tomorrow?"

"Six-thirty."

"I'll be ready," Amanda responded with a smile, suddenly feeling very happy as she got out of the car.

The next twenty-four hours winged by unbelievably fast. Before Amanda realized it, she was dashing down the stairs to meet Jarod. This time there was no tension in the conversation. They talked easily and on varied subjects during the drive to the restaurant. She found he could exert a vast amount of charm. During their meal she became impressed with his keen sense of humor. By the time it was over, she knew there were no doubts remaining that she was confusing her teen-age infatuation with the attraction he held for her now.

"Where are we going now?" she asked when he escorted her from the restaurant to his car.

"You," he emphasized lightly, "are going home."

Amanda glanced at her watch. It was barely nine o'clock. As if he had read the question that sprang into her eyes, Jarod added, "I'm leaving early in the morning and I have some work to do before I leave."

"Oh, I see," she murmured uncertainly. The next question rushed out before she could stop it. "When will you be back?"

"Saturday, I hope. Why? Will you miss me?" His eyes mocked her.

"Don't tease, Jarod. You know I will."

"Why do you think I would know that if you don't tell me?" They were inside the car and he switched on the interior light so he could study her face.

"You always seem so certain." Self-consciously she brushed her hair from her face.

"I never seem to feel so certain when it comes to you. Perhaps that's why you intrigue me so."

"Are you going to Pennsylvania again?" She swallowed.

"Yes. I'll try to be back by Saturday night. We

may yet have our date on a Saturday." His fingers closed over her hand. "Do you have to huddle against the door?"

"I'm not," she protested.

"You're an awfully long way from me. Come on, sit over here," he commanded. The gentle pull of his hold brought her beside him, his arm circling her shoulders while he nestled her head against his shoulder. Without indicating that she was causing the least encumbrance, he started the car and one-handedly reversed it out of the parking lot into the streets. "Do you know how long it's been since I've held you this close?" She felt the brush of his chin across the top of her head. "The last time was in your father's office."

A warm glow spread over her, her skin tingling at the remembered encounter. She resisted the impulse to snuggle closer and sighed contentedly instead.

"Did you enjoy yourself tonight?" Jarod asked softly, his hand caressing the upper part of her arm.

"Yes." The affirmation came out in a soft whisper.

"What are you going to do while I'm gone?"

"Why?"

But he ignored her query. "If I have any problems, I may not be back by Saturday. I'll call you in that event. All right?"

"Of course," Amanda agreed, unwillingly recognizing that they had made the turn onto the street where she lived.

Reluctantly she started to straighten when Jarod

braked the car to a stop in front of her house and turned off the engine, but a softly spoken "no" halted her movement. Long brown fingers cupped the back of her head and bent it back to explore her mouth with his. The gold tips of her lashes were the color of the flame that encircled her heart while it pumped the throbbing fire into her blood. A blind, unending yearning had her quivering in his arms.

"Saturday is so far away," he murmured, his mouth moving against the side of her cheek, adding to her already feverish glow.

"Too far," she moaned softly. "Do you have to go?"

His teeth bit into the lobe of her ear, evoking a sensual pain of delight. "I've been asking myself that, but I keep coming up with the same answer. Yes, I do."

The steering column blocked her efforts to strain closer to the lean hardness of his body. His mouth moved relentlessly over her face, seeking her lips again and again with a violent urgency that left Amanda shaken and totally submissive.

"I don't want to let you go into that house," Jarod muttered savagely, tantalizing the curve of her lips with his. "You'd better go while I can still take my hands off you."

"Not yet," she pleaded, nuzzling the brown column of his throat when he raised his head from her, but his fingers dug into her shoulders and pulled her away from him.

"Now, Amanda!" The slender thread holding his control was visible in the tight clenching of his jaw while the harsh light of desire glazed in the dark eyes that possessively swept her face.

"All right." But her voice was shaking and uncertain, quivering like her body from the overwhelming passion of his embrace. From somewhere she found the strength to move to her own side of the car, her gaze clinging to his face, noticing his breathing was as uneven as hers. "I'll be waiting for you Saturday—whatever time you come back."

Jarod's fingers raked through his ebony black hair as he ripped his gaze from her face. "Don't say things like that, Amanda. Not now. Not even if you mean them. Just go. Get out of the car!"

The stinging lash of his voice whipped out at her. "I didn't mean to make you angry, Jarod."

"I'm not angry." But there was a growl of displeasure in his tone as his dark gaze flamed back at her. "At least, not with you. At myself, maybe, because I know in my gut that I can make you say yes. I'm not accustomed to taking cold showers, Amanda," he concluded dryly.

Her head tipped forward, the red gold strands of hair that fell forward matching the color in her cheeks. The wild singing of her heart echoed the truth of his words. A few more minutes under the arousing caress of his mouth and hands, and she might have begged for the satisfaction he promised. He was still an unknown quantity. She couldn't begin to understand why Jarod, who admittedly was used to having his way, should allow her to deny him.

"You will call if you can't be back by Saturday?'' Amanda couldn't hide her aching need for his touch as she turned her gaze helplessly toward him.

His arms spanned the distance between them, drawing her briefly to him while he pressed a fierce kiss on her mouth, then moved a breath away.

"I told you I would, honey. I don't say what I don't mean," he said. "Now will you please get out of this car. Don't make me touch you again."

He reached around her and opened the door, his action forcing her to step out. Amanda paused beside the car, staring almost hungrily at the dark face and the light of desire smoldering in his eyes.

"Hurry back," she whispered, and turned quickly away before she lacked the strength.

Before she reached the door of the house, he was driving away. After the comparative silence of the night, the house was alive with sounds. The muted sound of a radio came from upstaris, overshadowed by the voices coming from the television. Not quite ready to let go of the freshness of those moments of ecstasy in Jarod's arms for the mundane conversation of her family, Amanda slipped into the empty kitchen. As she absently poured a glass of milk, she heard footsteps coming toward the room. She glanced behind her to see her father appear in the doorway.

"Well, hello." There was surprise in his greeting. "You're home early again tonight. Anything wrong?"

"No." Self-consciously Amanda shook her head in a movement of negation. "Jarod has to leave early in the morning again. He'll be back Saturday."

"Will you be seeing him again?"

"Saturday," Amanda nodded. The gleam of amusement in his eyes induced a wide smile to spread across her face.

"You're not worried anymore about who he is?" he asked.

"No." She took a sip of milk, looking suddenly thoughtful. "Yesterday I said something about not having much in common with him. Do you know what his reply was, dad? He said a man with money isn't better than anyone else, he only lives better."

"I've always had the impression that his feet were solidly on the ground. I guess I was right." Her father smiled.

"I wish my feet were," Amanda sighed, then realized how revealing that statement was and glanced at her father.

"Are you falling in love with him?" he asked gently.

A wry smile lifted the corners of her mouth. "I think I already have," she admitted.

"You've heard all the gossip about him and all the women that have been in and out of his life, haven't you?"

Amanda laughed lightly. "Are you warning me about him after encouraging me to see him, dad?"

"I suppose I am." He shrugged and smiled, an arm circling her shoulders. "If he weren't interested in you, I know he wouldn't be seeing you. I don't want you to be hurt, though."

"I know." Her lips brushed his cheek fondly. She knew Jarod had the power to hurt her, but she didn't want to look any farther ahead than Saturday. "Tomorrow is another working day, dad. I think I'll call it a night."

"I imagine I'd be wasting my breath to wish you pleasant dreams," he chuckled.

"That's right!" Her brown eyes sparkled happily as she moved lightly from the room. "There aren't any other kind," she called from the hallway.

THE BLACK TELEPHONE stared back at her silently. Amanda readjusted the book on her knee and looked away, telling herself again that Jarod would be back on Saturday as he had promised and there wold be no need for him to call. But the closer it came to Saturday, the more apprehensive she became that something would happen to detain Jarod in Pennsylvania.

"We're going out to get a Coke, 'Manda." Her brother Brad slapped playfully at her leg, Cheryl Weston standing beside him. "Quit moping around beside the telephone and come with us."

"Tobe's coming, too," Cheryl urged, the expression in her eyes asking that Amanda make it a foursome so Cheryl wouldn't have to compete with Tobe for Brad's attention.

At that moment Tobe walked into the living room. Brad waved him to join them. "Use your influence with Amanda," her brother ordered.

"I don't feel like going out tonight," Amanda declared with a shrug, feeling the need to assert her own wishes before they snowballed her into agreeing.

Tobe took the book from her unresisting hands and tossed it on the table beside the phone, then joined her on the couch. His arm familiarly encircled her shoulders.

"Take big brother's advice," he said with a wink. "You can grow old sitting around waiting for the mighty Jarod Colby—you said yourself he wouldn't call until tomorrow. It's Friday night. Who wants to stay home on a Friday?"

"I do," Amanda insisted with a laugh.

"We're only going to be gone for a couple of hours," Brad urged.

"Maybe he'll find out you were with me," Tobe teased. "It might make him jealous."

"I am not interested in trying to make him jealous," she stated, firmly but gently taking the hand that was around her shoulders and raising it over her head so Tobe's arm was back at his side.

"We'll go somewhere and dance." Tobe didn't give up. "You like to dance. It'll be fun. Then maybe Cheryl will quit throwing daggers at me."

Cheryl darted him another angry glance before looking guiltily at Brad. "I do not," she defended herself, then added her plea to Tobe's. "Do come, Amanda. We won't be that late coming back."

"Amanda!" Her mother's voice inserted itself in the group. "You have a visitor."

All heads turned in unison. Amanda's heart gave a convulsive leap as her eyes encountered Jarod standing in the doorway to the living room, his features grimly taut with a cold glitter in his eyes. Despite the harsh look, she sprang eagerly to her feet, moving to him with unconcealed happiness.

"I didn't expect you tonight," she murmured softly, gazing into his face.

The hardness of his eyes flicked over Tobe before returning to her upturned face. "I finished sooner than I thought I would," he commented smoothly, that hated aloofness in his expression.

"Another fifteen minutes," Tobe spoke up easily, "and we would have spirited Amanda out of the house. It's a good thing you arrived now. She would have killed me if she'd found out you'd come while she was gone, and I'm too young to die."

"Would it really have bothered you if you had missed seeing me tonight?" Jarod asked in a cynical tone.

Her mouth opened immediately to assure him that it would, but her brother's voice broke in before she could speak.

"Is that an understatement! She hasn't set foot out of the house since Tuesday night except to go to work. Nobody's been allowed to be on the telephone longer than five minutes in case you tried to call."

"Bradley Bennett!" Amanda cried out in embarrassed protest, her gaze sliding self-consciously toward Jarod before it shifted to her parents who had been watching the proceedings with amusement. "Mom, dad, Jarod and I are going out on the porch."

Jarod stepped to one side. His hand touched her shoulder as she moved past him and stayed there as he followed her down the hall to the front door. Once outside, Amanda walked quickly to the railing.

"I hope you didn't get the wrong impression in there," she said nervously, a hand smoothing the hair along her neck. "My brother is always teasing me about my dates."

"Do you mean you didn't miss me?" Jarod asked.

Amanda pivoted sharply. "Oh, yes, I did." At his soft chuckle, she realized he had been teasing her and she colored at the quickness of her affirmation.

"If you'd said anything else, I would have strangled you!" A humorless smile pulled at the corners of his mouth. "In fact, I wanted to when I walked in the room and saw you sitting on the couch with that Peterson boy."

"He's like another brother to me," she murmured, her heartbeat quickening.

"He'd better be." There was just enough underlying roughness in his voice to let her know he meant it. In the glow of the moonlight she watched him cup a lighter to his cigarette, enjoying the sight of him after three long days of waiting for him to come back. "What does your family think about me?" Jarod asked, slowly exhaling a cloud of smoke.

"My younger sister is a little awed by you, but my brothers aren't the least impressed," she answered lightly, unsure why he was asking.

"And your parents?"

"They admire and respect you."

There was a sardonic curl to his mouth as he studied the burning tip of his cigarette. "Even though they know I have designs on their daughter?'' he challenged mockingly.

A fingernail trailed along the ege of the porch railing. ''Naturally they realize we're attracted to each other,'' Amanda dodged.

''Do you honestly believe they would condone an affair between two consenting adults if one of them is you?'' he jeered.

''No.'' Her voice was tight, the muscles of her throat constricted by pain. This was not the way she had expected him to welcome her. Her forehead drew together in a confused frown.

''And how do you feel about it?'' There was an underlining of harsh demand in his velvet tone.

''Jarod, please.'' Her head moved helplessly to the side. ''You're making it hard for me—''

''Hard for you!'' For all the quietness of his outcry, there was violence, too. ''I've gone thirty-six hours without sleep, cramming four days' work into a little less than three. I left my attorney to tie up the loose ends, caught a plane back to Atlanta and drove straight here because I couldn't stand being away from you another minute. And you still don't know the hell I go through every time I touch you. Hard for you!''

The last came out with a sound of contempt and disgust as Jarod tossed the cigarette into the dark and turned away. He was halfway down the porch steps by the time Amanda had recovered from his savage outburst.

''Jarod!'' Her trembling legs carried her after him. When her fingers touched his arm, he stopped. ''I'm sorry. You must believe me,'' she implored, her fingers curling into the sleeve of his jacket. There was no room for pride in her heart as the love that enveloped it welled up in her eyes.

For a full second, the hard glitter remained in his eyes. Then he sighed heavily and the harshness faded from his face.

"I shouldn't have snapped at you," he conceded. "I'm tired and—" a wry smile added emphasis "—frustrated. Nothing went the way I planned it tonight. First I find you sitting on the couch with that—"

Her fingers touched his lips to silence him. "Let's not go over it again," she whispered.

"Let's go for a ride in the car," Jarod suggested softly, catching her hand and holding it.

"Yes," she murmured—as if she needed to voice her agreement when she was already moving toward the car.

CHAPTER EIGHT

THE MOON WAS a silver crescent suspended above the pine trees. A smattering of stars winked in the purpling blue sky. Amanda had no idea where they were going, but she didn't care as her head rested comfortably in the hollow made by his shoulder and arm. For a minute this evening she had been certain Jarod was going to walk out of her life, and she realized what a crippling blow that would be. She couldn't suppress a shudder at the thought.

"Are you cold?" His head bent toward her as he slowed the car.

"No. I was remembering how close I came to letting you walk away tonight," she answered shamelessly.

He gradually edged the car onto the wide shoulder of the graveled road, stopping it beneath the overhanging branches of some tall pines, their heavy scent drifting into the car.

"You probably should have." He made a cynical sound in his throat as he reached out to turn off the motor. "Your instincts about me are correct."

"What instincts?" she teased, her hand sliding under his jacket across the thin material of his shirt.

The intimate movement forced a groan from Jarod's throat as his hand closed over her arm to halt the searching caress. A second of hesitation followed before he pushed her roughly against the back of the car seat, half turning to pin her there while the blazing light in his eyes raked her face and neck. But the trusting brown eyes that shone back at him exhibited no fear at his suppressed violence.

Her mouth throbbed to feel his kiss, her lips parting in anticipation of his touch. His hands held her arms at her side as he ignored the invitation of her lips to bury his face in the fiery locks curling around her neck. Jarod continued to hold her still, plundering the softness of her throat and shoulders and tantalizing her face with rough kisses on her eyes, cheeks, and ears until Amanda was turning and twisting her head to find his wandering mouth.

The kindled fire he had sparked burst into the searing flames of demanding passion when he finally allowed her lips to find his. The need for his possession of her screamed in every nerve end and she whimpered softly against his bruising lips whose touch instantly changed from frustrated ardor to deliberate, total mastery of the senses. He drew back against his seat, pulling her with him, allowing her hands to touch him in trembling caresses while his own moved intimately over her body.

Resistance was impossible. It never even crossed her mind to protest when his fingers undid the top button of her blouse and she felt his fiery touch against her naked skin. She was clay to be molded in his hands, totally submissive to every movement, willing to become whatever he wanted.

Slowly Jarod arched her backward until she was

lying prone on the car seat, the exquisite pressure of his lean body on top holding her there. As his legs slid intimately between hers, a shudder of mindless ecstasy quivered through her.

His mouth moved across her cheek, the warmth of his breath, uneven like hers, fanning her lashes. "I'll try not to hurt you, darling," he murmured against her skin.

The sound of his husky voice opened the last gate and released the torrent of love behind it. Her hands lovingly cupped his face to allow her lips to move over his.

"I love you, Jarod," she whispered, aching certainty in the shaking depths of her voice. "Shamelessly, completely, without end. I love you. I love you."

It took a full minute before Amanda felt the stiffness with which he held himself. Then her caressing fingers and lips felt the tight muscles of his jaw. In the next instant he was pushing himself away from her, unmindful of the hands that tried to hold him. Blank confusion reigned as Jarod opened the car door and stepped outside, his hands on his hips as he breathed deeply of the night air. Hurt and stumbling, she followed him, her fingers tentatively touching his shoulder while she tried to recover her wits.

"Jarod?" Her voice was questioning and puzzled.

The arm nearest her left his hip and encircled her waist, drawing her against the comfort of his side. But Amanda could feel the tenseness, the rigidity of his touch that made the hardness of his body unconsoling.

"What did I do?" She turned her troubled and pain-filled eyes to his face, unable to believe that the desire that had been carved in every line could disappear so quickly or be replaced by such unrelenting coldness.

"I want you." The skin of her throat burned where his fingers touched it even as his harsh voice struck coldly at her heart. "I want you, but I'm not going to lie, Amanda. I don't love you."

She gulped back the outcry of pain and looked blindly away from his face. Hot waves of humiliation and shame engulfed her. She tried to pull free of his arms, but he kept her there and she was too stunned and hurt to care.

"You don't care for me—at all?" she asked in agonizing softness.

"I want you," he said bitterly, "the same way I've wanted dozens of other women."

Her shoulders hunched forward. "You don't feel any difference with me?"

"What difference could there be?" Jarod mocked.

"Love."

"There's no such thing," he jeered. "Through the ages, lust has been disguised as love. Love doesn't last any longer than lust does, because they're the same thing. Love is a joke."

"That's not true!" she protested vigorously.

He chuckled derisively. "There's two divorces for every marriage. Is that your proof of lasting love?"

"What about the people who are together for thirty or forty years?"

"You sentimental fool! First they were trapped by children and mortgages and security. Then they became habits to each other and were too old and tired to break them."

"Oh, God!" Amanda felt sick to her stomach, unable to accept the scorn the man she loved was displaying.

"After a few months, you'll find that you don't love me," Jarod went on cynically. "The newness will wear off and I'll no longer excite you the way I do now. It's always the same."

"A few months," she moaned bitterly. "Is that how long most of your women last?"

There was a pause. "Yes."

"Even Vanessa." Her lips trembled as she said the name.

"Vanessa Scott? She didn't last that long."

"Yet you always go back to her," Amanda remarked numbly.

"Did she tell you that?" he mocked. "She wants to marry money. It's not me she's after."

"I can't believe I'm hearing any of this." Her hands moved to cup her ears. "I tell you that I love you and you laugh at me!"

"I'm not laughing. You've let yourself get carried away with your emotions and have started believing in something that doesn't exist," he told her harshly. "You want me and I want you, but don't build the desire you feel into romantic dreams."

"I love you, Jarod. The way I feel is no dream

that's going to fade in the morning. I thought I had no pride where you were concerned." She spoke softly but for the first time calmly. "If all you want from me is an affair, then the answer is no. If, as you say, all you feel is lust, I don't ever want you to touch me again."

His penetrating gaze scrutinized her expression. The tightening of his mouth acknowledged the conviction he saw written there.

"Very well," he said grimly. "I'll take you home."

"I feel sorry for you, Jarod," Amanda said numbly as she started to get into the car. "To not believe in love must make you the loneliest man in the world."

But his dark head moved as if he felt sorry for her because of her delusion. The light in his eyes mocked her as he slid behind the wheel. Amanda felt surrounded by a polar ice, stunned by the freezing grip on her chest. Each slow beat of her heart seemed to widen the crack that was slowly appearing in its walls. The pain was unbearable, too deep to be assuaged by tears as she huddled silently against the car door. Unseeing eyes stared out the window of the moving automobile. The only image that registered in her mind was Jarod's face, carved lines untouched by softness. Now she understood why. A man who felt no love could exhibit no gentleness.

IT WAS DAYS before the numbed shock wore off. And after them came a succession of more days when Amanda tried desperately to hate Jarod. If he had deceived her, she might have succeeded in her attempt. Instead she found her abiding love for him laced with compassion and even pity, because what meaning was there to life without love?

The searing heat of August promised that September was not far away. Amanda held on to her sanity by convincing herself that when September came, she would return to college and leave behind the images that haunted her. No more would Jarod's ghost appear in the living-room door as it had done on that last night, nor would his wraith-like form flit through the halls and ballroom of Oak Run. The tempestuous dreams of being smothered by his burning kisses might even end. But she didn't really believe the breach in her heart would ever heal.

At first her family had teased her about Jarod's absence after the marked attention he had paid her. Then they began to look behind her stoical replies and see the strain behind her smile and the dullness in her brown eyes, and his name was avoided. The unasked questions in her parents' eyes were the hardest to ignore. Only once did her mother ask what had happened. Amanda had shrugged and said they had quarreled, adding to stave off more questions that it was personal. Her parents held considerable esteem for Jarod as an employer and a man. Somehow she couldn't bring herself to destroy that, no matter how much he had hurt her. Vengeance wasn't part of her nature.

Beads of perspiration had collected on her forehead and upper lip as Amanda turned to wave her thanks to Linda, who had given her a ride home from Oak Run after her father had failed to come for her. A smile flitted across her face as she noticed the family car still parked in the driveway. He had probably become engrossed in a baseball game and forgotten the time.

As she mounted the porch steps, she could hear no blare of the radio. Only silence came from the house. As she swung open the screen door, the whirr of an oscillating fan came from the living room. There was no rattle of dishes or silverware, no odor of food being cooked for Saturday-night dinner, no voices, only the lonely whirr of the fan.

"Mom! Dad!" A puzzled frown wrinkled her brow as she walked down the hall glancing into each empty room. "Grandpa! Where is everybody?" Her path carried to the stairwell. "Bonnie, are you home?" Only her own voice echoed back.

A car door slammed in the front of the house and Amanda hurried back to the door. She reached the screen door at the same instant that a tall, dark figure strode onto the porch. The blood receded from her face, leaving an unnaturally white pallor to her skin.

"What are you doing here?" she whispered as Jarod opened the door and walked in.

"I went to Oak Run to pick you up, but you'd already left," he said as if that answered her question.

Her eyes hungrily devoured his face, reimprinting each ruggedly handsome line on her mind as if in the next moment she would be struck blind and his was the last face she wanted to see.

"What do you want?" she demanded as she

turned away before the temptation to melt into his arms would become irresistible.

"Amanda—" he began.

His hand reached out to grasp the soft flesh of her arm left bare by the ruffled gown that was her uniform, but she wrenched free of his hold, emitting a tortured cry. "Don't touch me! Don't come near me! Haven't you hurt me enough already?"

"Stop it!" This time his fingers held her shoulders in an iron grip from which she couldn't shake free. "Your father is in the hospital. I promised your mother I would bring you there as soon as I could."

Her struggles stopped. "Is this some cruel joke? Some devious new plan of yours?" she cried bitterly. Fear clouded her eyes as she stared into the unchanging, harsh expression on his face.

"It's no joke. The doctors think your father has suffered a stroke," he answered grimly.

"I don't believe you." Red gold curls fanned her cheeks as she shook her head vigorously. "How would you know what's happened to my father?"

Jarod breathed in deeply as if to control his anger. "I'm a director on the hospital board. We were touring the hospital this afternoon to make recommendations on updating the facilities. I was there when the ambulance brought your father in."

"No!" Her protest was a horrified gasp, but this time Amanda believed him.

"Don't get hysterical on me," Jarod ordered. He must have seen the panic forming in her eyes.

"He's alive, but his condition is critical. Your brother and grandfather are at the hospital now, but I think your mother needs a woman with her. Go upstairs and change out of that gown. Where's your little sister?"

"Bonnie?" she asked blankly, trying to gather her scattered wits and react with the calmness he possessed. "She's, er, she's working, I think.... She's a waitress at... at Shorty's Café. I... I can't remember what time her shift ends."

There was a frantic sob in her last statement and the pressure of his hold increased slightly in a silent command not to panic. "I'll call and find out while you change," he said firmly. He turned her around and pointed her in the general direction of the stairs.

After the first few faltering steps that Amanda took in compliance, tears began streaming down her face. She gathered the long folds of her gown in her hands and ran the rest of the way to her room. Her parents had always seemed indestructible, growing older without ever aging. She couldn't even remember them ever being sick. Now her father was lying in critical condition in the hospital. Her fingers were trembling so badly she couldn't unhook the back of her gown. Sobs of despair tore at her throat as she attacked the metal fasteners again.

"Amanda?" Jarod's voice came from the upstairs hall.

"I'm... I'm in here," she called weakly.

The door to her room opened immediately. "Bonnie left the restaurant about five minutes ago. She'll be here any minute," he told her.

"I can't undo these hooks," she murmured. The sight of his composure forced back the sobs as she quickly scrubbed the tears from her face.

Under any other circumstances Amanda would have been conscious of the swift sureness of his fingers as they unhooked her gown. Their touch would have inflamed her, but now she was only grateful for their steadiness. The need for haste pushed aside her modesty as she stepped out of the ruffled gown, letting it fall in a heap on the floor. Partially aware that her scanty undergarments left little to the imagination, Amanda accepted the pantsuit that Jarod had taken from her closet, avoiding his onlooking gaze.

"Hello! Where is everybody?"

With her clothes in her hand, Amanda ran to the door. "I'm upstairs, Bonnie!" she called. "Come up here."

Then she turned, the sound of her sister's footsteps on the stairs. Her frightened eyes turned to Jarod, needing the assurance of his self-possession to break the news about their father.

"Get your clothes on," he said quietly. The dispassion of his tone calmed the sudden acceleration of Amanda's heart at her sister's arrival.

"Where's everybody gone?" Bonnie demanded as she burst into the room, stopping short at the sight of Jarod standing in the center and Amanda just stepping into a pair of slacks. Bonnie immediately took a hasty step backward, her face coloring in embarrassment.

"Bonnie, wait!" Amanda called out, glancing

guiltily at Jarod as she realized how intimate the scene must look. "Jarod is here because—" she walked quickly to take her younger sister's hands "—daddy's...daddy's in the hospital."

Bonnie looked from one to the other in disbelief. "No!"

"I couldn't believe it, either, but it's true." Amanda stared down at the hands held in her own.

"Your father has had a stroke." Jarod walked up behind them and handed Amanda the rust print blouse that matched her slacks, a gentle reminder to finish dressing. "As soon as Amanda is ready, I'll take you both to the hospital so you can be with your mother."

"But daddy has never been sick," Bonnie protested. "You must be wrong!"

As her sister threatened to give way to the hysteria rising within her, Jarod stepped between them, his soft, husky voice gently admonishing her to remain calm, that her mother would need the strength of all her children. All the while his dark gaze kept track of Amanda's movements so that when she was ready to leave, he had already begun guiding Bonnie to the stairs.

At the hospital the two girls were shocked by the ravages of fear and grief that had aged their mother before their eyes. That numbed sense of disbelief seemed to hang like a cloud over everyone, including their grandfather, who sat hunched in a corner, a shadow of his former lively self, unable to accept that somewhere in the hospital his son was fighting for his life.

"How is he, mamma?" Amanda asked, extracting herself from her mother's tender hug and helping her to a nearby chair.

"I don't know," was the mumbled reply.

"The doctors are still with him." Brad was standing beside the chair, his eyes bright with unshed tears.

Her mother turned imploring eyes on Jarod. "Perhaps you could find out?" she asked anxiously. "I shouldn't ask you. You've done so much already."

"We've been all over that, Bernice." Jarod smiled, ignoring Amanda's look of surprise that he should address her mother so familiarly. "I'll see what I can find out for you."

Then he was striding away without waiting to hear the fervent thank-you from her mother. They all remained in huddled silence for long minutes before Amanda rose and walked to her brother.

"Have you telephoned Marybeth and Brian? Where's Teddy?" she asked in a low voice so her mother couldn't overhear.

"Jarod's already contacted everyone," Brad told her, shaking his head as if he couldn't believe it himself. "Mandy, I don't... I don't know what we would have done if he hadn't been here at the hospital. Mom just sort of went to pieces and grandpa—he hasn't said a word since we got here. And I wasn't any help at all. Mom kept crying and crying. Then Jarod showed up and took charge. He and mom went off in a corner until she finally stopped crying. I don't know what you and Jarod had a fight about, but whatever it was, he more than apologized for it today."

However futilely, her brother's words made Amanda's love run deeper. Knowing how Jarod's composure had kept her from falling apart and the way he had staved off Bonnie's hysteria, she knew his quiet authority had to have affected her mother the same way. This knowledge radiated in a glow of pride when he returned a few minutes later, bearing the news that the doctors believed her father's condition had stabilized.

"It will be a while before you're allowed to see him," Jarod told her mother, "but I think the worst is over. It might be permissible to shed a few tears of happiness now even if the danger hasn't completely passed."

Weak, laughing sighs of relief echoed through the room as they all said silent prayers of thanks. Yet none wanted to voice their jubilation aloud. As Jarod had said, the danger hadn't completely passed. Amanda's hand touched Jarod's arm, wanting to express gratitude for all he had done. She smiled tentatively as his dark gaze moved thoughtfully over her face.

"May I see you alone?" she asked softly. There was a slight inclination of his head in agreement and she turned to her mother. "We'll be back in a few minutes," Amanda assured her.

With a smile that was divided equally between them, her mother nodded her understanding and Jarod and Amanda walked from the small waiting room.

CHAPTER NINE

THE HAND SLIGHTLY RESTING on her back guided Amanda to the vacant sun room. Now that she was alone with Jarod, she felt self-conscious. She watched him light a cigarette and she gathered the courage to speak.

"I want to thank you for all you've done," she said hesitantly, her eyes downcast.

"Perhaps you should save your thanks until you've found out what it is that I have done." Before his voice had been persuasively soothing; now there was a brittle quality to it that brought her gaze up sharply.

"What do you mean?" she murmured, noticing the mocking glitter that appeared in his eyes.

"How familiar are you with your parents' financial situation?" he parried her question.

"What has that got to do with this?" Amanda frowned.

"Are you aware that everything they own is under second and third mortgages? Did you know all medical coverage has been cancelled? I'm certain you know they have no savings, not with four children in college. At this moment, the only money they have is the two weeks' sick-leave pay your father is entitled to receive from my company." Jarod paused to let the full gravity of the situation sink in. "In less than a month, there'll be no money to pay bills, provide food or shelter, nothing for the cost of the hospital, and no tuition money for you or your brothers."

"Oh, my God!" Amanda reeled from the almost physical blow of his words. She had never guessed how severe the repercussions could be from her father's attack. "Does mother know all this?"

"That was the main reason for her panic," he replied. "After she'd told me all this, I convinced her that my company would take care of everything. I didn't mention that whether Colby Enterprises carries it out or not depends on you."

"On me? Why does it depend on me?" she whispered, frightened by the ominous threat hidden in his words.

"Because—dammit!—I still want you!" Jarod snapped, grinding out his cigarette in an ashtray.

Her stomach lurched sickeningly. "So what are you asking?" She was surprised that her voice could sound so calm. "Do you want me to become your mistress?"

"I would be satisfied with that arrangement," he admitted satirically. "Unfortunately it would only be a matter of time before your parents found out, and I think they would have qualms about taking money from their daughter's lover."

Amanda turned blindly away, her mind searching wildly for another way to come up with the money that would be needed.

"I wouldn't have to return to college. Brad has

enough saved for his first term's tuition. Maybe Teddy does, too, and Brian,'' she said frantically.

"Even if you were able to take care of that, it wouldn't solve the problem of the bills and payments and medical costs, not counting what it would take to live," he jeered. "Not even Tobe, who comes from a fairly wealthy family, would be able to loan or give your family enough money to keep it going, particularly since his parents don't approve of his relationship with yours." There was a sardonic light in his eyes as they glittered complacently over her. "Believe me, I've considered all the possibilities that might be open to you as alternatives to my offer. If you want your family to retain its status quo, Amanda, you'll have to come to me."

She shivered at the calculating coldness in his voice. "How can you expect me to agree to become your mistress?"

"I've studied your family. You possess one of those trite, old-fashioned relationships of all for one and one for all. Sacrifice is second nature to all of you. With your father lying in a hospital bed, neither you nor your brother would think twice of setting aside your education to rally around the family hearth and protect it." Amanda could tell by the derision in his tone that he considered such action foolhardy and unworthy of praise. Jarod wasn't admiring their closeness; he was making fun of it. "Your brothers will find that it's much easier to leave college than it is to return after a few years' absence. Their future rests on the outcome of your decision about my offer."

"To become your mistress," she repeated, throbbing pain making her words tremble.

"My mistress, my wife, whatever you want to call it." Jarod shrugged with a gracefully arrogant movement.

"Wife?" Amanda stared into the cold bronze of his face.

"I thought I'd already explained." His expression mocked the confusion in her eyes. "That vain family pride wouldn't allow your parents or your brothers to accept charity from your lover, but if I were your husband and a member in good standing, they wouldn't think twice."

"So you're asking me to marry you?" Amanda asked, needing to hear the statement in order to believe it.

"Yes," Jarod answered without any show of emotion. "Aren't you in love with me anymore, or have I proved to you how fickle and fleeting desire is?"

For one charged second, she had almost believed that he was going to admit he loved her, that he had found their separation unbearable. To him, she was only the grapes just out of reach, the sweet tender grass on the other side of the fence. He had once told her that he always got what he wanted. The thrill was in the chase. Once she was his, in body as well as in spirit, the excitement would be gone. As he had put it, the newness would fade and he would be ready to discard her for another.

"If it takes you so long to answer," he jeered softly, "perhaps you're finally realizing that love is an illusion with no substance in fact."

Amanda couldn't meet his derisive eyes. "Love exists, Jarod. I was so blinded by love for you that when you deceived my mother, I mistook your cruel treachery for kindness."

"It was not deceit if you say yes," he reminded her cynically.

Bitter gall rose in her throat. "You know you've left me with no choice."

"Only because you want me. If you found me repulsive, you wouldn't consider my proposal, not even for your family." A finger tilted her chin upward so he could look into her face.

"Please, don't humiliate me anymore." The sun-gold tips of her lashes fluttered over her brown eyes, shutting out the painful acknowledgement that what he said was true. She started to turn away.

"Not yet." His arm reached out, blocking her movement. His fingers touched her arm in a light grip that she knew could instantly become like steel should she try to leave after he had ordered her to stay. "Our discussion isn't over."

"Discussion?" It was Amanda's turn to jeer. "Isn't my agreement to anything you suggest merely lip service?"

"More or less," Jarod agreed complacently. "But I want you to become adjusted to the fact that we'll be getting married next Saturday. Naturally we'll wait until tomorrow to inform the rest of your family."

"Saturday?" she breathed. "That's impossible! How can you insist on such a thing with my father so ill?"

"Your father has survived the attack. True, his condition is critical, but he'll recover. If you're harboring any foolish notions that you aren't going to marry me until your father can walk down the aisle beside you, you'd better change your mind now. It will quite likely be months before he would be recovered to that point, and I will not wait that long," he told her with brutal candor. "Since our marriage is a farce, a celebration would be hypocritical. A small wedding with the immediate family in attendance is all we require to put the seal of legality on our affair for your parents' benefit. Under the circumstances everyone will understand our reason for keeping it simple, and with your father in the hospital we'll be spared the idiocy of a honeymoon."

"You have it all laid out like a battle plan. Every opposition is anticipated in advance." Her stomach churned sickeningly as she stared at the ruthless man who was soon to be her husband. "Like General Sherman, you destroy everything in your path until you achieve your objective. After Sherman reached Savannah and the sea, he remained only a few months—or was it two or three—then he turned his armies in another direction, seeking another victory elsewhere."

"Nothing lasts forever, Amanda," he said bluntly, not at all upset by the sarcastic sting of her voice. "You can reconcile yourself to the fact that in a few months you'll be free of me and my plundering Yankee ways. What's a few months out of your young life?"

"Marriage really means nothing to you, does

it?'' she murmured, amazed that he could already be plotting to be rid of her.

"No. And that shocks you, doesn't it? A piece of paper or words spoken in a church can't change the fickleness of human nature. There's the difference between you and me. You are a romantic, trying to change what can't be changed, and I am a realist, accepting what can't be changed.''

"And children? Don't you ever want children?''

An indefinable something flickered across his face at her question before the mask hardened.

"No. Procreation is not one of my desires,'' he snapped. "Do you have any more questions?''

"No, none,'' she answered, shaking her head sadly.

"I saw the doctor go in to speak to your mother. Shall we join them?''

The stroke, a severe one, had left her father partially paralyzed and deprived him temporarily of his speech. He regained consciousness that evening and the family was allowed to see him for short intervals. Jarod Colby was a law unto himself. His entrance into the restricted room with Amanda wasn't questioned by any of the hospital staff any more than it had been questioned by her family.

Amanda's heart turned over at the sight of her father's lanky frame covered with a bed sheet and surrounded by various tubes and monitoring devices. The worst was trying to summon an encouraging smile as she stared into his brown eyes glazed with fear. The sight of the previously indestructible figure lying helplessly in the bed constricted her throat until the simplest greeting couldn't squeeze through. Jarod's arm moved around her waist as he almost physically carried her the last two feet to her father's side.

"Hello, Sam," Jarod said quietly. "Or perhaps I should call you father, since your daughter has finally agreed to marry me."

Her eyes darted to the aquiline profile in surprise. Jarod had said they wouldn't tell the family until the next day. Then she felt the questioning eyes of her father turned on her for confirmation. Jarod's fingers bit punishingly into her waist when she hesitated.

"It's true, daddy." Her eyes filled with tears, whether from the futility of her own love or from the pain induced by Jarod's grip.

"I don't want you to worry about a thing," Jarod instructed her father in that quietly authoritative tone of one accustomed to taking charge. "We're all family now. I'll take care of everything until you're back on your feet."

The nurse on duty in the room blinked at the pair in surprise, but Amanda didn't notice. The frightened look in her father's eyes had dimmed as his eyelids fluttered down and a small breath of relief slipped from his pinched lips. She knew then that his fear had been for his family and not his own welfare. There was satisfaction in knowing her action had relieved that burden. Instinctively she raised her eyes to Jarod to thank him for putting her father's mind at rest. But in the arrogant bronze mask, she saw that this was all part of his plan. He was manipulating all their emotions to serve his own ends.

"We'd better let your father rest now," he said, his eyebrow arching at the sudden flare of anger in her eyes. Amanda moved quickly out of his grasp to the hall, brought up sharply by the hand that yanked her back to him. "What's wrong with you?" he demanded, keeping his voice low so that the scene between them appeared quite intimate.

"You're using us. You're using all of us without any regard for our feelings or our pride," Amanda accused bitterly.

"You will all be receiving compensation." His mouth moved in a cold smile.

"I hope someday your plans come crashing down on your head!" Her whole body trembled with the resentment boiling inside. Hate—the black side of love—was showing its face.

But Jarod only chuckled. "My poor little red-haired witch. Are you trying to prophesy my doom?"

"You can't have your way all the time. I only hope I'm there when you finally can't have what you really want."

"Will you pick up the pieces, I wonder?" he asked with a bemused smile, his hand reaching out to close over her throat while indicating how frail and insignificant was her spite. His touch frightened and excited her. It burned while it left her shivering from the cold thought of the time when he would tire of her. Dark, indolent eyes caught the paradoxical emotions that chased each other over her face. "Fiery Amanda, do you see how ambivalent your reactions are already becoming toward me? Right now you can't make up your mind whether to kiss me or claw me."

It was true. She couldn't. Then he stepped away and she could do neither.

IN THE WEEK that followed, Amanda was exposed to the many facets of Jarod's character. With her brothers he became the older brother, establishing a camaraderie while gently exerting his authority even as he gave the impression he was consulting them. Her mother looked on his as a wise counsel; he placated her fears with one hand and smoothed the way with the other. Even her grandfather stopped making snide comments about Yankees. Where there was disorganization, Jarod organized. Indecision was swept aside by his decisive action. He never explained, yet people were always left with the impression he had. Charm, diplomacy, compassion, authority, loyalty all surfaced at some time.

Amanda had thought he would flaunt his generosity, buy his way into the family, but strangely Jarod handled the transaction of money in such a businesslike way that no one saw a reason to speak of it. She marveled at the ease with which he persuaded others to go along with his suggestions, never issuing ultimatums or reminding them in any way of the power he held as head of Colby Enterprises.

It was ironic that Jarod was also honest. If he hadn't been, she would have succumbed to his considerable magnetism in the belief that he loved her. She wondered which was the worst hell—having an affair with a man, then finding out he didn't love her, or marrying a man knowing he didn't love her?

Light was caught by the arc of gold metal on her finger. There was no longer any reason to make imaginary comparisons. She was Mrs. Jarod Colby, for better or worse. At the moment it felt worse. But it was fear. Amanda felt the tenseness knotting her muscles, nerves so raw that the feather-lightest touch on her skin made them scream.

Standing in front of the altar with Jarod at her side, she had repeated the marriage vows that to her had always been sacred. The quiet clarity of Jarod's voice had made her heart ache. He had sounded so sincere, yet when her hopeful gaze had turned to him, there was no expectant light of tenderness in his jet dark eyes, only a possessive glitter that seemed to brand her as his. Until the ceremony everything seemed to have been moving at triple time. Now it had suddenly ground down to half speed.

The filmy net curtain slipped from her fingers. The only thing visible was her own reflection staring back at her from the window pane. The sleek satin sleeves of her robe felt as chilling as the apprehensions that enclosed her heart. Knowing there was no bond of love between them was beginning to make her believe that the ceremony and the marriage license meant nothing; and knowing that any minute Jarod—correction, her husband—would walk into the bedroom didn't ease the emotional turmoil that brought wary shadows to her brown eyes.

Except for the coolly indifferent kiss Jarod had given her at the wedding, he had not touched her. That was another thing she couldn't understand. He professed to want her so much, yet he hadn't shown the slightest bit of emotion or desire. Her hands rubbed her arms, trying to rid herself of the shivers that trembled over her skin. A flush of shame colored her cheeks as she wondered how she could possibly meet Jarod's eyes. In retrospect, Amanda could see he had bought her, paid a high price for her. Tonight was when he would inspect the merchandise.

"Are you afraid of the dark, Amanda?"

The mocking voice spun her away from the window, her fingers automatically sliding up her mud-green robe to clutch the top more tightly together. She had thought her hearing was attuned to the sound of water running in the shower of the adjoining bathroom, but the uneasy wanderings of her mind must have blocked out the signal of its stoppage. Every light in the muted gold bedroom was on, an attempt by Amanda to take away the dominance and intimacy of the turned-down bedclothes.

Jarod's question hung in the air as her wide eyes stared at the unbearably short toweling robe wrapped around his middle. The bronze tan of his face was repeated in the same dark shade over the rest of his body. The broad chest with its thick cloud of curling black hair tapered to slim hips and a flat stomach. The sinewy muscles in his thighs and legs seemed coiled, waiting for the command to carry him across the room to her. Waves of crimson red suffused her entire body as her apprehensive gaze encountered the twisted smile of amusement on his face, signaling that he was aware of her scrutiny. Amanda pivoted back to the window, her breath coming in jerky gulps of near panic.

"What induced that becoming blush?"

The gold carpet didn't betray the sound of his movement, but the snapping sound of a light being switched off warned her he had moved. There was another click and another light went off, leaving only the lamp beside the bed. Then her nose caught the clean scent of soap behind her and she stiffened.

"Are you embarrassed because your friend Cheryl told me of your infatuation for me as a girl?" he mocked softly, his voice coming from over her right shoulder.

Her head dipped slightly as she remembered the mortification she had felt when Cheryl had blurted out the story of Amanda's schoolgirl crush at the small reception after the wedding. Never would she forget the cynical amusement that had danced in Jarod's eyes.

"Must you bring that up?" she demanded in a grudging murmur, her fingers nervously raking back the red gold hair that had fallen forward.

"The night of the cotillion I sensed that your resentment of me had nothing to do with my supposedly superior status in the community. Yet I couldn't imagine that the incident of my rudeness you related could have had such an impact. It never occurred to me that I could be an object of idolatry to a young girl," he mused thoughtfully.

"Don't remind me what a fool I was!" Amanda protested, blinking back the acid tears that burned her eyes.

"Surely your dream came true. Didn't you marry me this afternoon?" Jarod taunted her.

She turned sharply around to voice her remorse for the empty vows they had exchanged, vows that were twisting knives of regret in what was once her heart. But she hadn't realized how very close he was to her. The few inches that separated them made the impact of his virility all the more potent, smothering her until she couldn't catch her breath.

Her gaze flew upward to the dark, enigmatic face indolently watching her. Amanda quickly averted her head, although she had lost the power for further movement. Unwittingly her gaze was directed to the bed and she shut her eyes tightly against the sudden vision of Jarod's raven black hair contrasting with the whiteness of the pillow.

"I can't go through with this," Amanda whispered weakly. "I thought I could, but I can't."

"Why?" She had expected arrogance or anger, but certainly not that note of amused curiosity in Jarod's voice. "We made a bargain."

"Yes, but—oh, don't you see?" Her eyes were round and pleading when she looked at him, her fingers tightening their hold on her robe. "You don't want me. I'm only something you paid for and now you feel you must use to receive your money's worth."

Not a word of denial came from his lips. "How did your astute mind reach that conclusion?" As he continued to tower above her, there was an air of satisfaction in his expression, as if he were glad she had made the discovery.

"Oh, Jarod, I'm not totally ignorant." The aching words scraped her already raw throat. "In all the times we've been together this past week, you never once indicated that you ever wanted to touch me, let alone make love to me."

"Would you have preferred that I did?"

"Yes," she admitted softly, bowing her head to elude his penetrating gaze. "It might have made tonight easier for me."

The hand under her chin firmly tilted her head back so he could see her face. "Did you want to kiss me? Do you want to be held in my arms?"

"Yes." This time she didn't try to hold back the two tears that slipped from her lashes as his hand lightly rested on her shoulders.

"Why?"

"You know why," she answered in a tormented whisper, "I love you."

His hands moved over her shoulders, down her arms, to close over her wrists, gently tugging so that her fingers would release their hold on her robe before he drew her hands to his chest. His naked skin was fiery hot to the touch. The heat seemed to fuse her hands in place. Amanda didn't think she could have pulled them away if she had tried. She felt his fingers deftly untying the sash that held her robe in place.

"Why didn't you even kiss me once?" Her words came out cloaked in an agonizing moan as his hands slid around her waist, their touch burning through the thin fabric of the nightgown beneath her robe.

"Because I swore I would make you ache for me the way I have for you these past months." A savage black light blazed in his eyes. The mask fell away and she could see how tightly leashed his control still was as he pulled her roughly against him, his physical need of her more apparent. As always, the contact of his lean, muscular body dissolved all resistance.

"Jarod, please!" Of their own volition, her hands swept around his neck as he ravished the throbbing cord below her ear. "Please pretend that you love me, if only for tonight," she begged shamelessly, her lips moving in soft feather kisses over the rippling muscles of his chest. "Pretend that our vows mean something to you, too."

With incredible ease, he swung her into his arms and carried her the few paces to the bed, snuffing out the light once he had lain her on the sheets. As the weight of his body settled onto the mattress beside her, love and shame tore at her breast with equal violence.

His mouth brushed the side of her face. "I don't have to pretend. There was one vow that I will keep," Jarod declared huskily. "With my body I thee worship."

With a whimpering moan of surrender, Amanda turned her lips to him and yielded to the spreading fire of his touch.

CHAPTER TEN

THE HAPPY TRILL of a bird singing its song to the rising sun drifted into the silent room. Amanda shifted slightly in protest to its wake-up call. Instantly the arm around her tightened to prevent further movement and she became conscious of the even rise and fall of the muscular chest beneath her head. A deliciously warm sensation filled her as she watched her hand slide intimately over the flat stomach to the dark hairs on the chest that was her pillow.

"Jarod," she whispered lovingly to no one in particular, cherishing the sound of it as its use was exclusively hers now. "Jarod, Jarod."

She could have repeated it a thousand times, but she didn't for fear she might wake him. The languorous warmth of the strong arms that held her was too tenderly blissful to be ended by rousing him from his sleep. Carefully Amanda tilted her head back so she could look at his face, which appeared not nearly so harsh in repose. The desire to touch it, to let her fingertips explore the carved plains and hollows, became almost too much and she lowered her gaze, closing her eyes to snuggle deeper into the crook of his arm.

Then the hand that had been resting on her

shoulder slipped to her face. The lean fingers were so close to her mouth that she couldn't resist the slight movement required to brush her lips against them. But at the first gentle kiss, the fingers closed around her chin and Amanda was pulled upward in one swift movement until her head was resting on the pillow inches from Jarod's face. The bright light in his black eyes told her that he had been aware of every moment.

"Good morning." There was a faint shyness in her voice.

He smiled and leaned over to press a lingering sweet kiss on her lips, feeling them part immediately on contact with his before he moved back to study her thoroughly.

"That is the way to say good morning," Jarod informed her, a smile tugging again at the corners of his mouth. "Or at least the prelude."

"I didn't mean to wake you," Amanda murmured.

"Didn't you? Then why did you keep repeating my name?" His hands were beginning their wayward caress of last night, moving with tantalizing deliberateness over her spine and hips.

"I like it," Amanda responded softly, feeling the flames of desire rekindling.

"And last night?" He arched her closer so her could nibble on her white shoulder. "Was it satisfying for you?"

"Yes." She breathed in deeply. "Was it...for you?"

"No." At the hurt look that sprang immediately into her eyes, Jarod chuckled and used the weight of his body to push her back against the mattress. "Last night I was satisfied, but not this morning."

"I probably should be getting your breakfast," she said in a breathless little voice.

"Why?" His indifferent question was muffled by the hollow of her throat.

Her fingers moved lightly over the bare skin of his shoulders. "I suppose because that's something wives do for their husbands."

"Mmm, until the drudgery and monotony become too much and they end up sending the man off with a cup of coffee and a peck on the cheek," Jarod said cynically.

"Not all wives," Amanda protested.

"I forgot." His head was raised, allowing him to look darkly into her face, mockery in his black eyes. "You're still wrapped up in those romantic notions about husbands and wives and the happily ever afters."

"Don't make fun of me, Jarod," she insisted, her hands reaching out to hold his face. "I do love you. I can't help it if I never want to leave you, no matter how shameless I sound."

"You can keep your dreams, Amanda. I won't take them away from you," he murmured grimly. "Hold on to them for as long as you can."

"What made you so bitter?" Her heart was aching with the depth of her love and the certainty with which Jarod had insisted it would someday end.

"I'm not bitter. I'm realistic. And right now, I'm very glad that I can assert my authority as

your husband and tell you to stop talking!'' There
was a hint of a smile before his mouth closed over
hers.

"DID JAR—MR. COLBY say what time he would be
home tonight when he called, Hannah?'' Amanda
inquired as the housekeeper walked into the dining
room where Amanda was polishing the silver,
humming a happy tune to herself.

"No, he only asked where you were and what
time I was expecting you home,'' the older woman
replied, taking the pieces Amanda had finished
and placing them in the buffet. "And I explained
that you'd gone with your mother to the hospital
and that your father was being released today. You
were going to help her get him settled at their
home, but you would be here by four o'clock.''

"And he didn't give any other reason for calling?''

"No, he didn't, Mrs. Colby.''

A thrill still shivered over Amanda every time
the housekeeper addressed her as Jarod's wife.
Amanda silently wondered if she would ever tire of
it, then decided she was acting like a silly bride.
They had only been married three weeks. Such a
short time when she thought about it, yet it seemed
as if she had always belonged to him.

The secret fear that someday all this happiness
must come to an end she kept firmly pushed to the
back of her mind. Dwelling on it would only make
each hour more miserable than the last. She was
convinced that heaven and hell were a state of
mind and she was determined that the days, weeks,

or months she spent with Jarod would be heaven. The hell would be living without him.

Jarod chided her occasionally, telling her she was "playing house," but she had discovered that all she had to do was slip into his arms and turn her face up for his kiss and he "played house" with her. And the wild ecstasy of their lovemaking never diminished for her, nor seemingly for Jarod, either.

Since their marriage, there had been a few business dinner parties in which the wives were in attendance. She and Jarod would become separated for one reason or another and their eyes would meet across a room. Amanda swore her heart would never stop turning over each time she saw that special light that said he wanted to be alone with her.

A glance at her watch told her it was nearly four and she handed the last of the silver to the housekeeper. She began tidying together the rags and the polish and the papers.

"I'll take care of that," Hannah announced.

The housekeeper didn't object to Amanda's doing some of the extra tasks around the rambling house, but she drew the line at the simple chores of cleaning up, making beds, and doing dishes. Those came strictly under Hannah's heading. That had been a difficult adjustment for Amanda, accustomed as she was to doing all those things her entire life, but Jarod had stated that she wasn't there to replace his housekeeper. The truth was there was plenty of work to keep both women busy and a surprisingly friendly relationship had developed between them.

The hands of the clock moved past four and the telephone remained silent. Amanda hadn't realized how much she had been expecting it to ring. Jarod had never called her during the day before, one of the many little things that indicated that he didn't regard her as his wife. Only to a certain point was she able to fool herself that their relationship was idyllic. How could it be when all the love was one-sided?

With a heavy sigh, Amanda gave up her vigil near the telephone and started toward their bedroom, guided by the half-formed decision to shower and change before Jarod came home. The sound of the front door opening coupled with his voice turned her quickly to the foyer, a smile of happiness unconsciously lighting her face.

"You're early!" Amanda cried in delight the moment her gaze caught sight of the tall, dark figure turning to meet her. An older, balding man was standing beside Jarod with a briefcase in his hand.

Jarod's hand reached out to draw Amanda forward with that impersonal touch she had come to loathe. It always seemed to remind her that she was only one of many women he had known and unlikely to be the last.

"Amanda, I'd like you to meet my attorney, Frank Blaisdale," he introduced.

"Mrs. Colby, this is a rare pleasure. I've heard many compliments spoken about you, but none of them did you justice." A smile concealed the shrewdness in his pale blue eyes and Amanda guessed that many a client and opponent had been lulled by the older man's quiet charm.

"I think I'm going to pretend that you're not exaggerating, Mr. Blaisdale, and simply say thank you," she answered with a smile in return. Her gaze slid to Jarod. "Would you like coffee or drinks in the study while the two of you are working?"

"I won't be staying long, Mrs. Colby," the attorney inserted.

"Frank is here to witness your signature on some papers we need to sign," Jarod added in explanation, beginning the movement that would take the three of them to his study.

"My signature?" Amanda questioned with a puzzled frown.

"Yes. Actually we should have had the agreement drawn up before we were married, but Frank was out of town on other matters and wasn't able to get it completed until now," Jarod said, opening the door the walnut-paneled room and ushering her inside.

"Agreement?" She looked from Jarod to the bland face of the attorney.

"You're beginning to sound like an echo, Amanda." There was a hint of censure in Jarod's teasing tone.

"I'm sorry, but I don't understand," she murmured.

"It's really very simple, Mrs. Colby." The attorney placed his briefcase on the desk, snapped it open and withdrew three sets of documents, handing one to her and one to Jarod, retaining the third for himself. "This is what could commonly be called a marriage contract. It outlines your husband's agreement to be responsible for the medical costs of your father's illness, the continuation of his salary as an absentee plant manager, and the tuition, et cetera, for your brothers' college education. There are also provisions here for a lump sum cash settlement in the event of a divorce. Read it over and see if you have any questions.

The paper in Amanda's hand seemed to catch fire. Cold flames shot through the fingers that held it, the scorching icy tongues forcing her to push the heartless document on the desk top before she was completely immobilized by its touch. Her brown eyes were wide with torment as she turned them to Jarod, calmly leafing through the pages of the agreement in his hands. As if feeling her gaze, he looked up, surrounded by that remote air she always associated with him when he was concentrating on an important business transaction.

"Do you have any questions?" A cold piercing quality was in his eyes as he spoke.

"Is this what you want?" she demanded in a tortured voice.

"I don't see anything that's been omitted." His gaze shifted smoothly back to the document, ignoring the plea in her eyes not to go through with this. "We discussed all the items in here except the amount of the settlement. Is a hundred thousand satisfactory, or do you want more?"

The hard indifference of his voice made Amanda cringe. In desperation, she turned to the balding man. "Where do I sign?" she asked.

"As an attorney, I can't help but advise that you

read this over carefully, Mrs. Colby," he demurred.

"Please—" she choked back the pain that rose in her throat "—I'm sure it's quite satisfactory. Show me where to sign."

The attorney handed her a pen and indicated the places on the document requiring her signature. Each stroke of the pen cut a new slash in her heart, increasing her pain to an almost intolerable level. When her name was affixed to the last page, she pushed the pen away from her, mumbled an excuse, and fled the room.

Her wavering legs carried her swiftly to the bedroom, where she was able to lean weakly against a bureau while heaving sobs tore at her chest. Then the door that she had securely closed behind her was opened. Amanda didn't need to turn around to know Jarod had followed her.

Her back stiffened and she withdrew herself from the support of the bureau. Determinedly she lifted her chin, pride insisting she couldn't allow him to know the agony the callous agreement had brought. Yet she knew the torment was in her eyes.

"I...I—" she breathed in deeply "—I think I'll take a shower before dinner," she finished, not turning to face him as she took a step toward the adjoining bathroom.

"Amanda!" The leashed anger in his voice erased all desire to pretend he hadn't hurt her.

Her chin dipped in defeat, but she didn't turn around. "Jarod, how could you do this?"

"It was as much for your protection as it was for mine," he said grimly. Lithe, silent strides had brought him across the room to stand behind her.

"That horrible agreement—it makes what I feel for you cheap and degrading. I love you so much and those papers make it sound like an unfeeling merger." Amanda shuddered bitterly.

"You know it won't last," Jarod insisted with a shrug.

"What? My love or our marriage?" she demanded, spinning around to blink the tears from her eyes as she gazed at the tightly clenched jaw. "I know I'll go on loving you after you stop wanting me. From the start I've known that our marriage wouldn't last. It's enough to receive what little affection you're capable of giving me. But this agreement takes even that away from me!"

His hands took hold of her shoulders, the fingers digging into her flesh for a moment before she relaxed. "You're a beautiful woman, but in many ways you're such a child," Jarod sighed angrily, drawing her against his chest and holding her there while he stroked her red locks as one would comfort a child.

Her inner coldness made Amanda huddle closer to the warmth his body generated, the shelter of his strong arms offering her the only apparent security that was left.

"I can't change the way I feel, darling," she murmured firmly as he rested his cheek against the side of her head, "any more than I can change the way you feel. I've accepted that. I only wish that awful contract didn't exist."

"I never realized how sensitive—how easily hurt you are," Jarod mused, tightening the iron band of his arms. "Forget about the contract, Amanda. It's just another piece of paper."

BUT THE CONTRACT wasn't any easier to forget than their marriage license and vows. During the next three months Amanda understood the subtle strain it placed on their relationship. Behind every happy smile there was a shadow, silently reminding her life with him was on a day-to-day basis, never certain when she woke in the morning whether this would be the day Jarod decided he didn't want her any longer. There were times when she wondered where her pride and self-respect had gone, that she should so greedily savor every precious moment she spent with him.

In the mornings it was difficult to keep from reaching out to him to reassure herself that he was lying in the bed beside her and thus reaffirm that he still welcomed her touch. At least that had been so every morning until recently. Now she lay quietly in the bed, watching him dress, and waitng for the moment when he would walk over to kiss her goodbye.

"You're becoming quite a lazybones." Jarod smiled into the mirror as he adjusted his tie, his dark gaze alighting on the contrast of her copper hair against the white pillow.

"There's no reason to get up yet." Amanda smiled faintly back, her eyes filling with love at the sight of the strong, bronze features with their ingrained arrogance and compelling attraction.

"No, I suppose not."

"There's a chance of showers today. Don't forget to take your raincoat."

He walked to the bed, a mocking glitter in his eyes. "You still enjoy playing the loving little wife, don't you?"

Amanda swallowed hard. "Don't make fun of me, Jarod."

"You used to laugh when I said that," he reminded her gently, bending down to kiss her mouth possessively. As his raven black head moved away, his gaze throughly swept her face. "You look peaked this morning."

"No makeup. What time will you be home tonight?"

"I have to drive to Atlanta, so it will probably be around seven," he said, brushing the tip of her nose with his finger before he turned to walk away.

"Be careful!" she called after him, and received a last look over his shoulder as he walked out the door.

Amanda lay in bed visualizing the route that would take Jarod to his study where he would collect his briefcase and papers, then out to the living room where he would tell Hannah what time he would be home for dinner that evening, then finally out to his car. Only if the wind was in the right direction would she hear the purr of the engine signaling his departure.

This morning she heard nothing. Very slowly she swept back the covers and gently levered herself upright, swinging her feet to the floor. Her legs were shaking badly, but she made it to the bathroom before the waves of nausea couldn't be held back any longer and she began retching.

When the last wave had passed, she clung weakly to the sink, fighting the weakness that threatened to buckle her knees. A succession of deep breaths helped her regain part of her strength and she turned to reenter the bedroom, only to find Jarod blocking the door, his eyes furiously dark and narrowed.

"Why didn't you tell me you were ill?" he demanded, eliminating the distance between them in one stride and sweeping her up into his arms to carry her into the bedroom.

"I...I didn't w-want to worry you," Amanda stammered.

"From now on," he growled as he placed her on the bed, "I'll make the decision as to whether you're going to worry me or not. Stay here and I'll go tell Hannah to fetch you some hot tea."

Her mouth opened to call him back, but her voice refused to cooperate until the door was closing behind him. By that time it was too late. Turning her head into the pillow, she began to cry, using the softness of the pillow to muffle her sobs. Several minutes later Hannah walked into the room carrying a cup of hot tea, not saying a word, but the look in her eye was speaking very eloquently as Amanda avoided her gaze to mumble a thank-you.

The teacup was drained and she was about to leave the warm luxury of the bed when she heard voices in the hall. Her gaze darted anxiously toward the door just as it opened and Jarod walked in followed by a tall, thin man. Her heart did a somersault of fear. Only a man of Jarod Colby's wealth and status could arrange for a doctor to make a house call, and the man was undoubtedly a doctor, as was confirmed a second later.

"This is Dr. Simon—my wife," Jarod introduced them.

"Good morning, Mrs. Colby. Your husband tells me you aren't feeling well today." The doctor walked briskly forward, but Amanda paid no attention to him.

"I don't need a doctor," she protested quickly. "It's nothing."

"We'll let Dr. Simon be the judge of that." Jarod's dark brows were drawn together in an uncompromising line.

The doctor started to reach for her wrist, but Amanda drew her hand away. "Please, Jarod, I have to talk to you," she demanded.

"After the doctor has completed his examination."

"Let me take your pulse, Mrs. Colby."

"No! Please, I'm not ill. I mean, not really." She glanced anxiously from the doctor to Jarod standing at the foot of the bed.

"You gave an excellent impression of being sick," he said as he motioned to the doctor to continue.

"Jarod, please, I want to talk to you—alone. I don't need a doctor."

"Will you stop behaving like a child?" he snapped.

"Very well." Amanda took a deep breath, then let her eyes seek his in a silent apology before she continued in a calmer and quieter voice. "I'm not acting like a child. I'm acting like a woman *with* child."

The silence after her announcement threatened to continue as Jarod stared at her in angry disbelief. Fortunately the doctor spoke up.

"Have you seen a doctor yet, Mrs. Colby?"

"Yes." Amanda nodded, not taking her pleading eyes from her husband's face. "My parents' doctor. It's all been confirmed."

"Congratulations, then," he said hesitantly. "I'll, er, leave you two alone."

CHAPTER ELEVEN

AT THE SOFT CLICK of the closing door, Amanda rushed to explain. "I tried to tell you several times, Jarod, honestly. I never wanted you to find out this way. I'm sorry."

"You're sorry!" he jeered, his lip curled to let her know how ineffectual her apology was. "My God! I never thought you would resort to this kind of trickery in an effort to hold me!"

"No. No!" The second exclamation was more vehement in her denial of his accusation. "That wasn't my intention at all!"

"It wasn't? Then why were you keeping it from me?" An explosive kind of sarcasm was written in his face.

"Because I knew you'd told me you didn't want children. That's why I was afraid to tell you. I never dreamed you would think...." Tears ran freely down her cheeks. "Jarod, I want this baby. I know I'll never be able to have you, but the baby will be part of you and it will be mine. Part of you will be mine. Don't you see?"

His head moved to the side in a gesture of wry cynicism. "Yes, I can see how your romantic heart could reach such an absurd conclusion. Do you expect my help in bringing up this child?"

"I expect nothing from you, Jarod," she answered quietly. "If you want, when we're divorced, I'll change my name and the baby's back to Bennett. I'll bring up our child with all the love and tenderness that's in me."

"For a while," he said dryly. "Then he'll get in your way. You'll find another man who won't be very willing to take on the responsibilities of another man's child. What will you do then? Ship him off to a bunch of boarding schools to get him out of your hair? Conveniently forget the child exists except at holidays when you remember to send him a present?"

"No, his childhood won't be like yours. That I promise you."

"What do you know of my childhood?" he snapped.

"Only the bits and pieces I've picked up from Hannah." Amanda couldn't meet the coldness of his gaze and tilted her chin downward. It would be of little use to tell him how many comparisions she had noticed between Jarod's childhood and Tobe's.

"Spare me your pity, because I don't need it," Jarod snarled savagely. "My lesson in the reality of life came early. I was never blinded by things that didn't exist. Santa Claus, the Easter Bunny, and love, they're all a farce, perpetuated by people without the guts to look life in the face. I never wore rose-colored glasses and I've never been sorry I didn't."

His words were like a thousand tiny paper cuts, setting her nerve ends raw with pain. "If you never dream, then you'll never have a dream come true," she whispered.

"You may have a point there." The sarcasm returned to his voice. "Because you've certainly had one of your dreams come true."

"What do you mean?" she gasped half-afraid of his answer.

"I mean we'll be staying together until after the baby is born."

Jarod pivoted sharply to leave and Amanda sprang from the bed to place a restraining hand on his arm. "No! I don't want to stay under those conditions," she protested.

She hadn't expected his reaction to be so swift. He spun her around, a hand closing over her throat as if he wanted to strangle her. Black fury raged in his face.

"Do you think you damned Johnny Rebs have cornered the market on honor and pride? I'm not the kind of man to get a girl pregnant and then throw her out. The one spark of decency that remains won't let me."

"Jarod." It was difficult to talk with his hand choking her throat. "I want to stay because you want me. Do you still want me?"

The hard diamond sharpness of his gaze raked her face in cold assessment. He could feel the throbbing of her pulse beneath his fingers and see in her brown eyes the pleading question that silently demanded his honest answer. His hand slid from her throat to the back of her neck as he pulled her roughly against the solidness of his chest.

"You're going to stay with me until the baby is born," he said hoarsely.

"I haven't strength to leave unless you push me away," she admitted in an aching whisper. The hard contact of his body was evoking that seemingly never-ending desire for his possession of her. "I have to know if you still want me."

There was no answer except the bruising crush of his mouth against hers, grinding her lips against her teeth while his hands moved in punishing caress over her body, fighting the material of her thin cotton gown. The pain was sweet agony as he swept Amanda off her feet and carried her to the bed.

Her fingers curled into the thickness of his raven hair and he buried his mouth in her neck and muttered, "Yes, yes, I do want you." For once Amanda was grateful for his brutal honesty, because she knew he spoke the truth.

IN THE MONTHS that followed, Jarod avoided any mention of the baby, even when her stomach thickened to a proportion that couldn't be ignored. More of his evenings were spent away from the house, drawing questioning comments and looks from the housekeeper. Amanda couldn't bring herself to ask if he still wanted her. His answer was all too obvious in his actions. But there was comfort in the life kicking vigorously inside her, although it would never replace the blissful sensation of Jarod's arms around her, a feeling that wasn't enjoyed as her time grew nearer.

The click of her knitting needles competed with

the tick of the clock as Amanda wondered whether Jarod would be home for dinner or would call at the last minute to say he was detained and that she should eat without him. Her answer was in the opening and closing of the front door. Unwillingly her eyes strayed to the living-room archway, a gnawing hunger for the sight of him eating into her heart. Then he appeared, a closed, emotionless expression on his face as he ignored her greeting to walk to the bar and pour himself a drink.

"How are you today?" His clipped question betrayed his lack of interest in her answer.

"Fine," she answered, swallowing the lump in her throat to concentrate on the partially completed green sweater. She could feel his brooding gaze watching her.

"It isn't necessary for you to make clothes," Jarod said suddenly. "If you need more money, ask for it."

She closed her eyes briefly at the savageness in his voice before answering calmly, "I enjoy it. It gives me something to do." An uneasy silence followed her statement. The baby kicked as if to remind Amanda of its presence. "I...I've been thinking a...about names for the baby," she said hesitantly. "Michele if it's a girl and David if it's a boy."

"What am I supposed to say?"

"I thought you might...want to make a suggestion," she ended lamely, unable to counter the contempt in his voice.

"Name it whatever you want," he growled, rising from the leather stool at the bar.

"Will you be eating here tonight?"

His gaze flicked derisively over his shoulder at her. "I don't recall mentioning that I would be going out, so I must be eating here."

"I didn't know." Her shoulders moved in a defenseless shrug. "You've been so busy lately, I thought perhaps you'd be gone tonight, as well."

"If you want to know if I'm seeing another woman, why don't you come right out and ask me?" His eyes blazed in anger at the flash of pain across her face.

"I don't want to know," she murmured, hating the weakness of her love, which allowed her to be the whipping boy.

"Wouldn't you enjoy chastising me for my lack of fidelity?" he jeered.

The knitting was thrust onto the couch as Amanda rose to her feet, trying to make a dignified escape from his stinging insults.

"Damn!" he muttered savagely, easily covering the distance to her before she could reach the hall. "That was a vile thing for me to say, Amanda." His hands closed over her shoulders, shaking with soundless sobs of torment. He pulled her against him, his mouth moving over the back of her head. "I'm sorry," he murmured.

"It's all right," she whispered. It didn't seem necessary to add that she understood why he had sought the pleasures of another woman. Her shoulders felt the deep shuddering breath he drew.

"I'll be leaving in the morning for Philadelphia," Jarod said, his hands releasing her shoulders as he stepped away. "I'll be gone about a week. You can tell Hannah that while she's packing my clothes, she might as well move the rest of my things into the guest bedroom. I'll sleep there from now on.''

Her mouth opened to protest, but she closed it quickly, glad her back was still to him and he couldn't see the agony his announcement brought. She murmured a quick agreement, and this time he didn't try to stop her when she rushed from the room.

''HELLO, MANDY DEAR, how are you feeling?''

Amanda blinked her eyes open and stared into the beaming face of her mother. A small sigh of pleasure slipped from her throat.

''Exhausted,'' she murmured in return, levering herself into a sitting position in the hospital bed. ''Have you seen the baby yet? Isn't he adorable?''

''All seven pounds and two ounces of him,'' her mother answered, nodding agreement.

''He may be three weeks premature,'' her father inserted, his speech still slightly slurred from his stroke, ''but he has enough hair to pass out to the other three babies in the nursery.''

''And it's all coal black just like his father's.'' Amanda commented and smiled contentedly.

''We reached Jarod about an hour ago,'' Mrs. Bennett said. ''He'll be flying straight back from Philadelphia. I know you must be sorry he wasn't here with you when little David was born.''

''I don't mind.'' Amanda lowered her gaze to the bed sheet so her parents wouldn't see the brief flicker of pain. ''I can't exactly visualize

Jarod pacing the floor in the waiting room, can you?"

"No, I suppose not," her mother laughed then let her hand reach out to her daughter's. "The nurse asked us not to stay long so you could get some rest. We'll be back to see you later today."

Amanda's eyes fluttered shut almost the instant her parents left the room. It seemed as though only a few minutes had passed before she heard the gentle voice of a nurse telling her that they would be bringing her baby in to her.

As the small bundle was placed in her arms, Amanda knew a joy that was beyond expression. A whole new world opened up at the sight of those tiny little hands wrapped in puny fists, flailing the air while the baby sucked vigorously on the nipple of his bottle.

Once his hunger was satisfied, he slept contentedly in her arms while Amanda gently pushed the silky fine black hair that covered his head into a semblance of order.

"My beautiful David," she crooned softly, lightly touching the button nose of the still red face. "I will try to love you as much as I love your father." An adoring smile beamed from her face. "I don't think it's going to be very difficult. I bet you're even going to have his beautiful dark eyes."

A sound from the doorway drew her attention, a look of regret forming in her eyes in anticipation of the nurse who would soon be coming to take the infant back to the nursery, but it was Jarod standing there instead, tall, imposing, and vaguely withdrawn.

Instinctively Amanda stretched out her hand to him. "Jarod!" Unbounded happiness shone in her voice. "I didn't think you would be here so soon."

His supple strides brought him to the side of the bed as he impersonally took the hand she offered. "Are you all right, Amanda?" he asked blandly.

"Yes." She couldn't help smiling; she was much too happy. Liquid brown eyes were turned back to the baby sleeping in her arms. "Isn't David the most beautiful baby you've ever seen?" Her gaze slid back to Jarod, trying to gauge his reaction to his son in the black steel of his eyes.

"Excuse me, Mrs. Colby," a nurse spoke quietly from the end of the bed. "It's time to return your son to the nursery."

Jarod released Amanda's hand and stepped away as she reluctantly surrendered the infant to the nurse. She watched the woman walk from the room before her gaze was pulled back to her husband. He was staring at her with brooding thoroughness. Self-consciously her fingers went to the tousled crimson gold hair, not knowing the curling disarray was attractively complementing the ethereal pallor of her skin.

"I must look terrible," Amanda proclaimed with a smiling grimace. "My hair is a mess and I have no makeup on."

But there was no affirmation from Jarod that he thought her beautiful. Her self-derogatory comment went completely unheeded.

"Dr. Henderson told me you would be released on Tuesday. I'll make arrangements for a nurse to move into the house Monday so she'll be there when you and the baby arrive home."

"No!" Alarm registered briefly in her face before she added firmly, "I'll take care of our son myself."

"Very well," he replied, clipping off the ends of his words bluntly. "Whenever you get tired of the role as little mother, you can hire a nanny yourself."

A great deal of her happiness vanished at his cynical sneer. "There's something you don't understand, Jarod," Amanda said tightly. "Our son isn't a toy and I'm not ever going to get tired of him."

"As you wish." There was a derisive move of his shoulders beneath the dark blue jacket. "I'll let you rest." Without even a goodbye he walked from the room, leaving behind a black cloud to dim the sunshine of her spirits.

DAVID'S WHIMPERING CRY woke Amanda instantly. It still amazed her how her ear was tuned to every sound coming from the crib, no matter how deeply she slept. Streaks of gold shimmered on the eastern horizon and the hands of the clock indicated half-past six, feeding time according to the hungry baby's tummy. Amanda slipped quickly from beneath the covers, tugging on her mud green robe as she hurried to the crib before David's stirring increased to a full wail of demand.

"Here, little man," she whispered, slipping a pacifier into his mouth, "I'll go and heat your bottle and be right back."

Quietly Amanda shut the door behind her, glancing hesitantly at the closed door of Jarod's bedroom. She could never look at without realizing there was more than walls separating them; and that knowledge hurt. Not for the first time was she grateful for the arrival of their son, who had brought a new purpose into her life. And right now that little boy was hungry, she thought wryly to herself as she hurried silently down the hall to the kitchen.

The water had just begun to boil in the pan holding the baby bottle when she heard the muted cry from her bedroom. The pacifier had evidently been lost.

"Just a couple more minutes, David," Amanda murmured aloud as she tested the formula and found it almost lukewarm.

By the time the milk was warmed and she began hastily to retrace her path to the bedroom, the cries had stopped. Assuming that by some miracle David had retrieved his pacifier, she didn't give it a thought until she opened the bedroom door and saw Jarod holding him in his arms, gently rocking the baby and looking as if he had done it all his life.

"I didn't mean to take so long," said Amanda, recovering her surprise and looking at the impatient wriggling of the infant before Jarod's dark gaze could capture hers.

"I was awake anyway," said Jarod, starting to turn to hand the child to her.

There was only a second of hesitation before she thrust the bottle toward him. "Would you feed him?'' she asked quickly, childishly crossing her fingers as she lied. "I dropped one of the bottles on the kitchen floor. Hannah isn't here yet and I'd like to clean it up before it starts to dry."

She nearly forced the bottle into Jarod's hand before she hurried from the room, not stopping until she had reached the kitchen, where she wrapped her arms around herself and smiled.

"You're certainly grinning like the cat that ate the canary," Hannah mumbled as she walked in the kitchen door. "Don't tell me little Davie's alarm clock didn't go off this morning?"

"Oh, yes, it did," Amanda laughed, nearly dancing over to the housekeeper and hugging her tightly.

"What's wrong with you, girl?" The usually sternfaced housekeeper let a smile of bewilderment tug at her mouth.

"Jarod is in the bedroom feeding David right now," Amanda whispered, as if saying it louder would bring the walls crashing down.

"It's about time, I'd say," the woman declared with a vigorous nod of her pepper-colored hair. "The little feller is more than a month old. He should know what it's like to be held by his daddy."

"I knew Jarod couldn't resist him forever," Amanda sighed, ignoring the sting of criticism in the housekeeper's statement. "I hadn't better overdo it the first time, though. With my luck, David will burp all over his robe. Fix some coffee and bring it up to my room, will you, Hannah?"

The contents of the bottle were nearly gone

when Amanda returned to the bedroom. Without a word she took the baby from Jarod's arms, a shy look of pleasure in her eyes as she looked at him.

"He's already burped," he said blandly.

"Not on you?" she asked anxiously.

"No."

Jarod stood beside the crib, watching with indifference as Amanda tucked the blanket around the contentedly sighing infant. Covertly she tried to glimpse a hint of pride or affection in the arrogantly set features, any sign that Jarod felt something for their son resting in the crib. There seemed to be nothing, yet she couldn't help venturing a comment.

"Sometimes it's difficult to believe that he's our son," she said softly. "That you and I made—"

"Don't waste your romantic nonsense on me, Amanda," Jarod snapped. "Keep it for that baby you're so proud of."

Her eyes rounded in disbelief at the savage rejection in his voice. A faltering movement of her hand brought her fingers in contact with the terrycloth sleeve of his robe. A ray of hope twinkled dimly.

"Jarod..." she began hesitantly. "You...you aren't jealous of our...our son, are you?"

"Jealous!" There was a contemptuous sound in his throat as the full force of his glittering cold gaze was turned on her. "To be jealous I would first have to care. And I don't care." The words were drawn out with emphatic slowness. "You and the baby could leave today and I wouldn't miss you at all."

Her whole body jerked as if he had slapped her, twisting her head to the side as she reeled from the shock of the pain. Incapable of speech, she said not a word, although painfully aware of his footsteps taking him out of the room. Her hands crept up to her face while the last of her hope died an agonizing death as bitter tears streamed down her cheeks.

"Don't waste your tears on the likes of him." Hannah's angry voice sounded from behind her. "He isn't worth it."

Amanda spun around, pride briefly halting her sobs. "Don't say that!" she gasped, more in terror because her mind was saying the same thing.

"It's the truth. And don't you be trying to put me in my place, either. I heard every word he said, and it would serve him right if you left this very day!"

"I love him." Amanda's face crumpled beneath the onslaught of tears. "It's so humiliating to love someone as much as I love him. What am I going to do?"

"The first thing—" the housekeeper drew her to the bed "—is for you to drink some of this coffee while I pack your things. It's time the high and mighty Mr. Colby found out how empty this house is without you. We'll see how good the food tastes when he sits at the table alone, and how sterile the house seems without a few women's things strewn around."

"It won't work, Hannah." Amanda shook her head dejectedly. "I knew when he married me that he didn't care for me. I only hoped that he might care about David. I told Jarod I would leave when he told me to go, and that's when I'll leave."

"What do you think he said a minute ago? Where's your pride?"

"I have no pride," she admitted wryly, roughly wiping the tears from her face. "You'd better take the coffee in to Jarod."

"I'll throw it in his face if I do," the housekeeper growled. "The ungrateful pup!"

"Hannah—"

"All right, I'll take it in to him." Hannah stiffly picked up the tray she had carried into the room. "But the minute he leaves, I'm getting your suitcases packed. And if I have to lend you some of my pride, I will, but you'll be gone from this house when he comes back tonight!"

"Oh, Hannah, I adore you," Amanda declared in a half laugh. "But I'm not leaving today."

"We'll see," the older woman sniffed, and walked briskly to the door.

CHAPTER TWELVE

THE DOOR CLOSED with a resounding bang behind Jarod as he entered the house, his impatient strides carrying him directly into his study. Tossing the thin briefcase on the leather sofa, he began shifting through the mail on his desk while lean, tanned fingers tugged at the knot of his tie. At the light rap on the door, his cold gaze glittered long enough in that direction to identify the person in the doorway before it returned to its task.

"What do you want, Hannah?" he demanded sharply.

"I was wondering what time you wanted dinner tonight."

"I have an appointment in a half hour, so I won't be eating here. You'll have to check with Mrs. Colby." He tossed the mail on the desk and made a half turn away from the housekeeper in silent dismissal.

"Mrs. Colby isn't here." There was the barest ring of triumph in the woman's voice.

Jarod glanced over his shoulder, a slight frown knitting his forehead as his penetrating gaze attempted to detect the reason for that peculiar tone of defiance. "What do you mean—she isn't here?" He challenged her for a more accurate statement.

"I mean she's gone." The woman's thin nose seemed to pinch together into a narrower line. "And more power to her, I say!"

Jarod appeared to weigh her statement, assessing it and discarding it as he again turned his back on her. "I don't believe you," he said with marked indifference.

"You don't have to believe me," the woman declared with a shrug. "But if you look, you'll find her clothes and the baby's are all gone."

For a moment, blazing dark eyes bored the fiery tip of their steel into the unflinching woman before Jarod shoved her out of the doorway and let his long, swinging strides carry him into the master bedroom. A sweeping search confirmed the housekeeper's statement, yet even when the physical search stopped, his gaze moved relentlessly around the room.

"There's no need to worry, Mr. Colby," Hannah said dryly, her less hurried steps bringing her to the open door. "The only things that are gone are personal possessions. She left the house just as she found it—cold and empty."

"I've had enough of your insolence!" Jarod clipped.

"Have you now?" A sparse brow arched above unblinking eyes as Hannah folded her arms in front of her. "Maybe I should quit and we can see whether or not you miss me. If you want to know where she's gone, she went back to people who care about her and the baby. Her family."

"Why should I care where she is?" His dark head was arrogantly thrown back. "It was only a matter of time anyway, since you seem to be so familiar with my personal life."

"I'm neither deaf nor blind."

His lips were pressed tightly together to hold back the angry retort. "You may leave, Hannah. As I have other commitments this evening, there's no reason for you to stay."

THE RELAXED INTERCHANGE of voices, casually discussing unimportant topics, seemed to insulate Amanda from the pain in her heart. She hadn't realized how strained her nerves were until she had stepped into the loving atmosphere of her parents' home. Drawing strength from their invisible blanket of security, she was able to match their light-heartedness and reacquaint herself with the joys to be shared because of the baby now being rocked gently in her grandfather's arms.

All of the family had gathered in the living room, including Tobe and Cheryl. The dinner dishes were done and her mother was sitting in the large chair beside Amanda's father, darning a pair of Ted's socks, smiling as she listened to the teasing exchange between Tobe and Brad, who had finally proposed to Cheryl. The slamming of the front door caught everyone by surprise, silencing their voices as they all turned as one to face the hallway.

Jarod's tall frame filled the doorway, a harsh expression etched over his drawn features, a suggestion of pallor beneath the teak brown tan of his face. With the cutting quality of a laser beam, his eyes pierced through Amanda, pinning her to the sofa and not allowing her to move.

The only one not stunned by the aura of explosive anger surrounding him was her mother, who calmly set her darning aside and rose to her feet.

"Jarod, this is a surprise." The cold glare of his gaze as he brought it to bear on her mother didn't silence her as it was meant to do. "I hope you haven't come to take Amanda home already. Since little David has been born, it's so rarely that she comes to visit us. I couldn't believe our luck when we persuaded her to stay for dinner."

Amanda's heart beat in an uneven rhythm as she watched Jarod stare at her mother, his head drawn back as if her words had caught him by surprise. Then his dark gaze swung on her, relentlessly searching her face while Amanda frowned her bewilderment.

"What's wrong, Jarod?" His continued silence prompted her mother's question.

There was a massive rise of his chest as he breathed in deeply, a hand raised to let his fingers tear through the sides of his hair. His head made a negative movement as if to shake off the demon driving him.

"I'm sorry," he mumbled, turning away to walk back the way he had come.

Amanda met her mother's questioning gaze with a blank look, but Jarod's abrupt departure brought her to her feet, as confused as the rest of them over his strange behavior. She hurried down the hallway after him, reaching the screen door before it closed behind him and catching him as he reached the top of the porch steps.

"Jarod, what is it?" Her voice slowed his steps, finally halted by the touch of her hand on his arm. "What's wrong?"

In the dim moonlight she saw him glance down at her hand. When he spoke, his voice seemed to come from some deep cavern.

"I'm taking you home, Amanda."

"Of course, but can't you tell me what's wrong?"

She sensed the indecision, something she found difficult to associate with him—Jarod, who was always so positive about what he wanted. He turned very slowly and the light from inside the house illuminated the ravaged pain in his face.

"I believed you'd left me." He spoke clearly and distinctly, revealing none of the agony that was written in his expression.

"I have neither the strength nor the pride to do that," she answered with a wistful smile. Then a curious thought fluttered on fragile butterfly wings in her mind. "Why would it matter to you if I did?"

"I deserved that," Jarod muttered, roughly grabbing her and crushing her against his chest. Beneath her head she felt the strong beat of his heart while he rubbed his cheek against her head. "I didn't believe it mattered. I thought you could leave me and I wouldn't miss you. Until tonight."

Weakly she clung to him, gasping at the unbelievable happiness exploding inside her while tears of joy streamed from her eyes. She had ceased hoping that she could ever mean anything to him.

"My love, my love," she whispered fervently. "And you thought those things you said to me this morning had sent me away from you?"

"No." She could feel the shake of his head as he tightened his arms around her, molding her ever closer against his trembling length. "It never seemed to matter how much I laughed at you or scorned the way you felt for me, you always stayed. I didn't think this morning would be any different."

"Then why?" Her head moved back, sending the long coppery hair cascading over the sleeve of his coat. "Why did you think I'd left?"

"Hannah told me you were gone." His eyes seemed to drink in the radiant glow of her face.

"But she knew I was here. She even phoned me to let me know you wouldn't be home for dinner."

"That scheming witch!" Jarod chuckled, a brilliant light entering his dark eyes. "She's the one who told me you were gone—for good. She even went so far as to remove all your clothes from your room to convince me."

"Oh, no!" Amanda cried with a gasping laugh. "No wonder you thought I'd left. She overheard what you told me this morning and was determined that I leave you. Jarod—" her eyes were shimmering with tears of apology "—I almost did. I was convinced that there was no hope for us, that you could never love me even a little bit."

One corner of his mouth twitched in a deprecating gesture. "I still don't know if what I feel for you is love," he admitted slowly and grimly. "When I look at you and see how your love for me has never faltered no matter how much I degraded you or mocked you, I tell myself I have to believe that such an emotion exists. All I'm certain of is that I don't want to face tomorrow without you."

"I won't ask for more than that, Jarod," she murmured, her fingers tracing the sensuous line of his mouth. The months of not touching him suddenly made her desire insurmountable.

"You deserve more than that." He pulled away from her touch. "You should have someone who will cherish you and thank God every day of his life that he has you."

"But it's you I want." Amanda smiled. Her hands curled around his neck, dragging his head down to her mouth until she heard him groan before he claimed her lips, his arms swinging her off her feet as he lifted her to a new height of love.

It was many minutes before her feet touched the porch floor, both of them breathing heavily, their faces flushed with the desires they had aroused in each other. For the first time, the intimate touch of his hands exploring her face, neck and shoulders was tender and loving, not driven by animal passion that would end in possession.

"I should have guessed what was happening to me," Jarod mused thoughtfully, gently folding her in his arms. "That night I met you, at the cotillion, and you refused to let me take you home, I told myself it didn't matter, that you were just another girl. And the next day I found myself at the planta-tion asking you to have dinner with me. I was going to have that scarlet-haired ghost who had haunted my dreams. When I discovered I had an innocent child, I was furious." His silent laughter at the thought fanned her hair. "I was determined to forget you existed, that I hadn't felt the yielding of your body at my touch. Then by pure chance I stopped at the mill and I knew you would be the one who would come to pick up your father. But you frustrated me again."

"Then you brought Vanessa to Oak Run and I was so jealous," Amanda remembered, and Jarod's arms tightened around her in reassurance.

"I don't know whether I was trying to prove to you or myself that you meant nothing. When you agreed to go out with me and I realized how much I disturbed you, I thought I would finally have you and get you out of my system once and for all." His voice was a low, husky caress. "Then you caught me off balance with your declaration of love and I insisted on having you on my terms or not at all. When we got married, I expected to become tired of you in a few months, but I discovered that I still looked forward to seeing your smile when I walked in the door and the darkness of night when I could take you in my arms."

"If that's true, why did you turn away from me?" her puzzled voice queried. "Why did you move to the other bedroom? Because I was pregnant?"

"Partly," he admitted wryly. "You must remember the scorn I felt for your avowals of love, and I couldn't reconcile myself to the seemingly unquenchable need for you. I thought if I deprived myself of you, the thirst would go away. But the more I denied it, the stronger it became."

"I thought it was David. I thought I had alienated you completely," Amanda murmured, slipping her fingers beneath his shirt to feel the strong beat of his heart. "I kept hoping that once you saw our baby, you would want him as much as I did."

"I guess you've found out what my childhood was like," he sighed. "Most of the other children I met experienced the same. I remember how it hurt to be always pushed aside by their mothers and fathers unless they felt like playing the doting parents, which was seldom. I taught myself early not to care for anyone but myself. Then you came along."

"I guess it all was meant to be this way. There were times when I was so ashamed of myself," Amanda said. "I knew I was letting you trample my heart and my love, and if I was any kind of a human being at all, I should leave you while I still had a little self-respect. But like a faithful dog, I kept coming back no matter how often you whipped me with your scorn."

Jarod suddenly crushed her against him, squeezing her so tightly that she could hardly breathe. "You don't know how it tears at my insides to hear you say that and know it's true." The admission was drawn through teeth clenched in self-contempt. "Even tonight when your mother made me realize that you hadn't really left me, I was ready to walk away and let you go on believing that I didn't want you. I would have left without ever telling you why I'd come. Still you ran after me, despite those vicious things I said to you this morning. And I knew I would never be able to live with myself if I didn't tell you the way I felt."

She tipped her head back, her lips parting to halt his flow of self-derision. Her breath was caught by the expression on his face. All his arrogance was gone, leaving the tender promise of love everlasting.

"There's something else I must tell you," Jarod said quietly. "Since the day I met you, I haven't been with another woman, not in the intimate sense of the word. If I couldn't have you, I didn't seem to want anyone else."

Two crystal drops hovered on her lashes as the last of her fears dwindled to nothing, and with a little gasp of sheer joy she wrapped her arms around his waist.

"I never thought I could be so happy," Amanda murmured, closing her eyes to savor the full ecstasy of the moment.

"Nor did I." His kiss touched her eye, her cheek, hovering below the lobe of her ear before it moved errorlessly to her mouth. "I think it's about time you took our son and your wayward Yankee husband home."

"Yes, yes," she repeated it again, more eagerly the second time.

Reluctantly he let her leave his arms, the expression in his face urging her to hurry back even though she needed no such encouragement as she dashed into the house and quickly gathered her own and the baby's belongings. The curiously amused glances of her family went unnoticed as she gathered David into her arms, wishing them all a cheery good night before hurrying back to Jarod. When she reached the porch, Amanda started to hand her bag and the baby's things to him, but Jarod pushed them aside.

"You drive home," he ordered, his carved features transformed by a smile that softened every corner. "David and I haven't had a chance to get acquainted."

A gurgle came from the blanket-wrapped infant as if he endorsed the statement, and both Amanda and Jarod laughed softly before the shining light of their eyes met. Gently Jarod gathered the baby in his arms.

"I love you, darling," Amanda smiled.

"I must love you, too," he murmured huskily, his dark gaze ardently returning the look in her eyes. A tiny fist pushed itself free of the blanket and Jarod looked down at it, offering an index finger that the little hand couldn't quite wrap around, although it tried. "Hold on, David. My cynical ways must be in the past, because I feel very proud of my handsome son." His gaze strayed to Amanda as he added softly, "And my wife, too."

Back by Popular Demand

Janet Dailey
Americana

A romantic tour of America through fifty favorite Harlequin Presents, each set in a different state researched by Janet and her husband, Bill. A journey of a lifetime in one cherished collection.

In July, don't miss the exciting states featured in:

Title #11 — HAWAII
    Kona Winds

#12 — IDAHO
    The Travelling Kind

Available wherever
Harlequin books are sold.

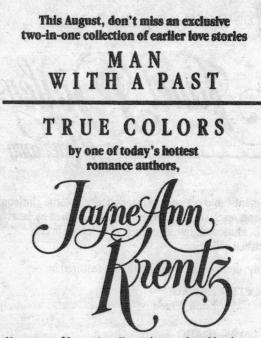